The grin dropped off Boris's face. "You tried to kill me, you son of a bitch."

"You were doing your fair share on that train, if you recall." Clint retorted.

"I suppose I did."

Clint nodded and resisted the urge to lunge at Boris right then and there. The simple fact that Boris hadn't moved from his spot or reached for his gun told Clint that he didn't want to make the first move.

"Tell me, Boris," Clint said. "Where's your bro—"

Clint's question was cut short as something heavy cracked against the back of his skull. The impact flooded Clint's head with dull pain as his ears filled up with the loud rush of blood. Soon, that rush was joined by the flow of air rushing past his face as he fell to the straw-covered floor.

DON'T MISS THESE
ALL-ACTION WESTERN SERIES
FROM THE BERKLEY PUBLISHING GROUP

THE GUNSMITH by J. R. Roberts

Clint Adams was a legend among lawmen, outlaws, and ladies. They called him . . . the Gunsmith.

LONGARM by Tabor Evans

The popular long-running series about Deputy U.S. Marshal Custis Long—his life, his loves, his fight for justice.

SLOCUM by Jake Logan

Today's longest-running action Western. John Slocum rides a deadly trail of hot blood and cold steel.

BUSHWHACKERS by B. J. Lanagan

An action-packed series by the creators of Longarm! The rousing adventures of the most brutal gang of cutthroats ever assembled—Quantrill's Raiders.

DIAMONDBACK by Guy Brewer

Dex Yancey is Diamondback, a Southern gentleman turned con man when his brother cheats him out of the family fortune. Ladies love him. Gamblers hate him. But nobody pulls one over on Dex . . .

WILDGUN by Jack Hanson

The blazing adventures of mountain man Will Barlow—from the creators of Longarm!

TEXAS TRACKER by Tom Calhoun

J. T. Law: the most relentless—and dangerous—manhunter in all Texas. Where sheriffs and posses fail, he's the best man to bring in the most vicious outlaws—for a price.

314

DYING WISH

J. R. ROBERTS

J

JOVE BOOKS, NEW YORK

THE BERKLEY PUBLISHING GROUP
Published by the Penguin Group
Penguin Group (USA) Inc.
375 Hudson Street, New York, New York 10014, USA
Penguin Group (Canada), 90 Eglinton Avenue East, Suite 700, Toronto, Ontario M4P 2Y3, Canada
(a division of Pearson Penguin Canada Inc.)
Penguin Books Ltd., 80 Strand, London WC2R 0RL, England
Penguin Group Ireland, 25 St. Stephen's Green, Dublin 2, Ireland (a division of Penguin Books Ltd.)
Penguin Group (Australia), 250 Camberwell Road, Camberwell, Victoria 3124, Australia
(a division of Pearson Australia Group Pty. Ltd.)
Penguin Books India Pvt. Ltd., 11 Community Centre, Panchsheel Park, New Delhi—110 017, India
Penguin Group (NZ), 67 Apollo Drive, Rosedale, North Shore 0632, New Zealand
(a division of Pearson New Zealand Ltd.)
Penguin Books (South Africa) (Pty.) Ltd., 24 Sturdee Avenue, Rosebank, Johannesburg 2196,
South Africa

Penguin Books Ltd., Registered Offices: 80 Strand, London WC2R 0RL, England

This is a work of fiction. Names, characters, places, and incidents either are the product of the author's imagination or are used fictitiously, and any resemblance to actual persons, living or dead, business establishments, events, or locales is entirely coincidental.

DYING WISH

A Jove Book / published by arrangement with the author

PRINTING HISTORY
Jove edition / February 2008

Copyright © 2008 by Robert J. Randisi.
Cover illustration by Sergio Giovine.

ISBN: 978-0-515-14405-5

JOVE®
Jove Books are published by The Berkley Publishing Group,
a division of Penguin Group (USA) Inc.,
375 Hudson Street, New York, New York 10014.
JOVE is a registered trademark of Penguin Group (USA) Inc.
The "J" design is a trademark belonging to Penguin Group (USA) Inc.

PRINTED IN THE UNITED STATES OF AMERICA

10 9 8 7 6 5 4 3 2

ONE

In most card games being played for big stakes, everything usually came down to the last hand. Unlike most games, where the players weren't exactly certain which hand would be the last, there was always something that cut through the air toward the end of the bigger games.

On this particular night, something crackled through the room that put out the sort of charge that could be felt before a lightning storm was unleashed from a dark sky. It was something that might not have meant much to most of the folks in Rick's Place, but the two at the round table in the corner sure felt the approach of what had to be the end of their game.

Clint sat in his chair, looking down at three nines, the king of clubs, and the five of spades. Making certain his expression didn't change any more than it needed to, he ran his fingers over the pile of chips in front of him. "I'll bet fifty," he said.

Olivia McKay was a trim woman in her late twenties who'd arrived in Labyrinth, Texas, just over a week ago. Her long, raven-black hair and slightly angled features showed a great deal of Chinese blood running through her veins. The dusky hue to her skin and the curve of her hips, on the other hand, hinted at the possibility of South American ancestry.

Clint had been trying to figure her out since her arrival, and the chance to play poker with her seemed like a perfect opportunity. But Olivia fancied herself as a gambler and seemed to have more than enough skill to back it up.

"Only fifty?" she asked. "Last time, you raised a hundred and the time before that it was eighty."

"Those times were bluffs," Clint replied with a subtle grin.

"The time before that wasn't. You were dealt two pair and bet two hundred."

"She's got you there, Clint," Rick Hartman shouted from his spot behind the bar.

Rick was a big Texan who was also the namesake of the saloon. Not only was he one of the more respected businessmen in Labyrinth, but he was also one of Clint's oldest friends.

"Keep your mouth shut and polish some more glasses," Clint hollered with just the right amount of disrespect.

Hartman knew better than to take those words at face value. Instead, he simply shook his head and waved Clint off using the old towel in his hand. "In that case, I hope she does clean you out."

"You're probably feeding her all the information she needs." Shifting his eyes as well as his grin toward Olivia, Clint asked, "Has he been telling you how I play?"

"He doesn't need to tell me anything," Olivia replied with a pretty smile that only made her slightly rounded face seem even prettier. "I've seen all I need just by playing with you this long."

"It hasn't been that long," Clint pointed out.

"Exactly."

Hartman walked up to the table while letting out a low whistle. "She's got you again, I'd say."

Clint kept his eyes on Olivia, but knew better than to leave himself open for more of Rick's barbed comments. "My bet's still the only one out there," Clint said. "And where poker's concerned, the money always has the final say."

When Hartman nodded this time, he shifted his eyes toward Olivia. "I'd say he's got you there."

Olivia didn't need to say anything when she glanced up at Hartman. Even though the Texan dwarfed her by standing near the table, he was the one to back up half a step with his hands raised as though he was being held at gunpoint.

"I won't stick my nose in anymore," Hartman said. "I was just making sure you had enough to drink." With that, he picked up the empty glasses on the table and took them back to the bar.

So far, Clint still hadn't taken his eyes off her. Considering the way Olivia's pale yellow dress clung to her tight curves, that wasn't exactly a chore.

"I'll call," she said with a shrug. After moving in the appropriate amount of chips, she picked up the deck beside her. "How many cards do you need?"

"Two," Clint replied.

She flipped him his cards and announced, "Same for me."

The game had started off with three other players, but they hadn't lasted very long. For the last few hours, it had just been Clint and Olivia. Since the game had been whittled down to these two players, the stakes had gone up considerably.

Having gotten rid of the two cards that weren't nines, Clint rearranged his hand while watching Olivia's face as she did the same. Although her smooth skin and long hair were easy on the eyes, there wasn't one thing on that pretty face to tell Clint much of anything of use where poker was concerned.

Olivia stared right back at him, wearing half a smile. "Are you going to pass the bet on to me?"

When he took a quick peek at his cards, Clint discovered

the two cards he'd gotten rid of had been replaced by the six and four of diamonds. "No, I'll do the honors. Three hundred."

Before Clint could move that many chips in, Olivia added, "Make it four."

Clint nodded. "Somehow, I knew you'd do that. How about we just make it six hundred and forty-nine?"

Olivia raised her eyebrows and ran the tip of her tongue along her upper lip. "That's all you've got left?"

"It sure is."

When Clint looked over to the bar, he saw Hartman leaning forward on both elbows and watching intently. "Can you believe this, Rick?"

"Stop talking to him and play," Olivia said with the same bit of fire in her voice that Clint had had when he'd been needling Hartman earlier. "I'm the only one you need to worry about."

"No wonder the others left," Clint said. "You're a hard woman."

"They left because they wanted a friendly game to pass some time," she replied. "I always play for blood."

"Do you now?"

She nodded, and then eased all of her chips into the middle of the table. "Yes, I do. Always."

"You've already got me on chips," Clint pointed out. "How should I cover this bet?"

"You could always fold," Olivia said with another sly grin.

Clint made a show of looking down at his cards and then shaking his head. "No. I don't think I'll fold. I do, however, think you're bluffing."

"Then what do you propose?"

"Double our original bet."

That widened Olivia's smile a bit. "You mean the one we made at the beginning of this game? The one before those other three showed up?"

"That's the one."

After thinking it over for all of two seconds, she nodded. "Done."

Clint smiled and showed his three nines. "You were drawing to try and fill in a hand," he said proudly. "You've got a cute little tell that showed up the last few times you were drawing for a hand and didn't have one."

Olivia let out a breath and set her cards facedown on the table. "You're right," she sighed. Then, she spread out her cards to show that all of them were clubs. "This time, I managed to fill in the hand I was after."

The confident smirk dropped off Clint's face. "Damn."

TWO

Within minutes of the end of that game, Clint and Olivia were in the hotel across the street from Rick's Place. They were in Olivia's room and she was currently sitting on the edge of her bed with her foot resting on Clint's bended knee.

"When I said I wouldn't mind getting you alone for an hour, this wasn't what I had in mind," Clint said as he remained on one knee at the foot of the bed.

"It wasn't?"

Looking down at the foot that was propped on his knee, Clint replied, "Well . . . not exactly." He reached up to slide his hands along Olivia's boot. The higher he moved his hand, the more her skirts fell away to reveal a tightly muscled calf. "Although I am starting to see the appeal."

"I bet you are. Besides, it's not just an hour anymore. It's two. Remember, I won that last hand."

Clint shook his head and reached up a bit higher under her skirts. Olivia's thigh was smooth as silk and warm to the touch. When his fingers glanced along the soft ruffle of her expensive panties, he slowly eased his hand back down.

"To be honest," he said, "I was only kidding when I

brought up that bet at all. I thought there was a good chance you'd slap me right in the face."

"Then why'd you mention wanting to get me alone?"

"Because there was the slight possibility that you'd say yes." Grinning, Clint unhooked the garter from her stocking and slowly rolled the thin material down her leg. "Actually, I was pretty sure you'd say yes."

"You mean that pretty little tell of mine?" she asked.

"Yep."

"What tell do you mean exactly?"

Clint shook his head and started unlacing her boot. "I'm planning on more games with you, lady. I'm not telling you my secrets just yet."

"Then maybe I'll take you up on that money you owe me."

"What money?" Clint laughed. "Those chips were just for show so we could see who won the game. That's why those other three left so soon. Poker's no fun unless you're playing for something."

"Oh, I was playing for something all right," she whispered. "And I'm claiming my prize right here. You get that boot off and do what I say. That's the deal, remember?"

"It wasn't the deal when we started," Clint pointed out. "All I said was I'd like to get you alone for an hour."

"That's before you lost so badly to me. Now you need to work off what you owe me." Gritting her teeth a bit and pressing her foot against Clint's chest, she said, "Now get to work."

Clint peeled the boot off Olivia's leg. The leather came up to her knee, but dropped away easily enough once the laces were loosened. He kept one hand on her ankle and used the other to toss the boot away. Clint then placed that hand on her calf and slid it all the way up.

"That's it," Olivia purred. "Now go higher."

Clint eased his hand up a bit more until he could feel those ruffled panties once more.   .

"Be careful," Olivia warned. "Those are expensive. Be gentle when you take them down."

Smiling up at her, Clint slipped his fingers under her panties to feel the smooth skin and soft downy hair between her legs.

Olivia closed her eyes and let out a slow breath as she leaned back a bit. "I told you to take them down."

"Yes, ma'am," Clint replied as he eased the panties off and slipped them over both of her feet. When he reached under her skirts again, he felt Olivia take hold of his wrist.

"Not yet," she said.

But Clint didn't let her move his hand. His fingers were already close enough to feel the heat of her body. Stretching just a little bit more allowed him to trace a soft line along the curve of her moist pussy lips.

Allowing him to linger there for another second, Olivia shook her head and pushed his hand away. "Not yet, I told you. Who won this bet anyway?"

"You did, but I think you cheated."

"Can you prove it?"

"No."

Smiling, Olivia took her foot from Clint's chest, placed her other foot in its place, and said, "Then get my other boot off."

Clint bit his tongue since he knew all too well he'd lost the bet. Then again, it was hard to complain about that since he was in a perfect spot to look up her skirts as Olivia lifted her leg so he could get to her boot. He took his time with the laces and savored the sight of the skin that was now bare since her panties had been removed.

"Here," she said as she pulled her skirts up and gathered them behind her back. "Now can you see a little better?"

Peeling off her boot and tossing it next to the first one, Clint said, "I sure can."

Olivia leaned back onto the bed, propped her heels

against the edge of the mattress, and spread her legs. "Now start making good on what you owe me."

As Clint unbuttoned his shirt, he said, "You are a bossy lady, you know that?"

"You love it," she replied with a warm smile.

"I don't know about that, but I may be able to work with it."

"You'd better. I didn't say you could take your shirt off," she snapped.

Clint couldn't help but flinch at the sudden shift in her tone, but his reaction had nothing to do with being intimidated. In fact, he was feeling something quite the opposite. Settling on the bed, Clint forced Olivia to back up a bit. Once she had her shoulders against the headboard, she smiled and rubbed her bent knees impatiently.

Then Clint made her wait just a bit too long, watching for her to glare at him before making his move. Just as Olivia was about to scold him again, Clint pushed her legs apart a bit more and then ran his tongue along the smooth curve of her pussy.

That single move took Olivia's breath away and caused her to grab a handful of Clint's hair. She hung onto him tightly so he wouldn't take his mouth from where it was.

"That's it," she groaned. "Oh, yes. Right there."

Clint slid his hands along her stomach and then reached up even higher. The neckline of Olivia's dress was low, but not low enough. Rather than rip the fabric of her blouse, he rubbed her pert little breasts through the material.

His tongue slipped inside her, driving Olivia to a shuddering climax. She pumped her hips against Clint's face before finally letting out an exhausted breath. When he shed his jeans and climbed on top of her, Olivia pressed her hands against Clint's chest as if to hold him back.

"What are you doing?" she asked playfully. "I didn't tell you to do this."

Clint wouldn't allow himself to be directed so easily this time. Instead, he grinned at her and shifted his hips until he felt the tip of his erection rub against her wet vagina. With one easy push, he slid inside her.

Olivia's eyes widened and she arched her back. Wrapping her arms around him, she closed her eyes and said, "You may proceed."

THREE

Two and a half hours later, Clint made his way across the street and back into Rick's Place. The moment Rick saw his friend stumble through the door, he poured a beer and chuckled.

"I told you she'd clean you out," Hartman said.

Clint stepped up to the bar and rubbed his neck. "I only wish every game I lost wound up like that one."

"She seemed like a handful."

"She sure is." After taking a long drink from his beer, Clint raised his glass and added, "Bless her heart."

Both of them shared a laugh and soon, Hartman had poured a beer for himself. The big Texan leaned against his bar and surveyed the saloon. "Looks like your game was all the excitement this place'll see for a while," he said. "At least for tonight anyway."

"There's a big tournament being held in Dallas," Clint told him. "All the gamblers will be headed there."

"Really? How do you know about that?"

"I heard about it in New Mexico just before I left to come here," Clint explained. "Everyone was talking about it, saying how there was supposed to be more money there than in the national treasury. Hell, even the side games could make or break a man."

Staring at his door as if willing customers to walk through it, Hartman grumbled, "Damn." He then shifted his eyes back to Clint. "I thought you loved poker. How come you're not at that tournament? Is it too late for you to enter?"

"Nah," Clint replied. "When I heard about it, everyone was still planning on what train they needed to take to get to Dallas. I believe the first games start tomorrow. Besides, it's not like they'll turn away my money if I decided to show up a little late."

"Then what are you doing here?" Leaning forward a bit more and lowering his voice even though hardly anyone else was in the saloon, Hartman asked, "That sassy little lady caught your eye that much?"

"Let's just say I was genuinely trying to win that game," Clint replied.

Hartman was laughing as he leaned back again. "I'd hardly call that losing, but I see your point. A smart man knows his limits."

"Hear, hear," Clint announced as he raised his glass for a toast.

Never one to leave his friend hanging, Rick raised his glass as well and took a drink. When he placed the glass down again, Hartman wiped some of the foam from his upper lip using the back of his hand. "So tell me, how'd you wind up getting on that lady's good side so quickly? There ain't a lot of men around here anyways—thanks to that damn tournament, I suppose—but every last one of 'em was eyeing Olivia."

Clint shrugged. "Eyeing a lady isn't usually enough to cut it. None of them stepped up to talk with her."

"That's it? You talked to her?"

"And I gave her a run for her money at cards. That seemed to hold more water with her than anything else. Of course, she may have been trying to divert my attention."

"From what?" Hartman asked.

"You recall that game she sat in on yesterday?"

"The one with those four cowboys from the Double Dutch Ranch?"

Clint nodded. "That's the one."

"What about it?"

"I caught her palming a few cards before I bought into the game for myself."

Hartman's eyes nearly bulged out of his head. "She's a cheater? Damn it, Clint, why didn't you say so? I don't take to crooked games being held at my place. You know that!"

Now, Clint was the one who glanced around at the other customers. At the moment, there were just a couple of drunks scattered about and a single game of gin being played at a table near the window. "Better keep your voice down, or you'll drive away your customers."

"Oh, they're not going anywhere," Hartman said. "I still got a bone to pick with you. If word gets out that I've started to allow crooked games . . ."

"There was no way you could have known what she was doing," Clint said.

"That makes me look even worse."

"She was playing for a pot that hadn't even reached ten dollars yet," Clint said earnestly.

Although Hartman relaxed a bit, he furrowed his brow in confusion. "She cheated at a friendly game? What's the purpose of that?"

"Who knows? She could have been practicing. She didn't even win the hands when she'd palmed those cards. Otherwise, I would have let you know all about it."

After contemplating that for a few more seconds, Hartman shook his head as though he had a bee in his ear. "I never did understand gamblers. Anyone who'd put their livelihood on the line in a game of chance has got a damn screw loose in their head."

"You play poker every now and then," Clint pointed out.

"Sure, but only in friendly games. Now, I'm not even sure about that. I hope you at least got that lady to stop what she was doing."

"I let her know she'd been spotted," Clint replied. "That seemed to be enough to get her to stop. After that, she tried to feel me out as to how I'd spotted her. Then, things sort of picked up from there."

Hartman laughed under his breath and refilled Clint's beer. "I'll say they did. How about you tell me all about her sweet little—"

"Excuse me," a young man with a dirty face said as he walked through the front door. "Which one of you is Rick Hartman?"

"That'd be me," Rick said. "What can I do for you?"

"I'm looking for the fellow who was playing cards over there," the young man said as he pointed to the table where Clint had been sitting a few hours ago.

As Clint squared his shoulders to the young man, he had no trouble spotting the gun hanging at the man's hip. Judging by the worn leather of the holster, Clint knew the pistol wasn't hanging there for show.

"That'd be me," Clint said.

FOUR

The young man narrowed his eyes and stared at Clint. His feet were already planted, and didn't budge as he reached for the gun at his side.

Clint could feel the muscles in his arms tensing reflexively as he waited for the man's hand to touch the holstered pistol. At the first hint the young man was about to draw, Clint knew he could clear leather and fire his own modified Colt. After that, the only question in Clint's mind was where he wanted the bullet to go.

Judging by the look on the young man's face, Clint didn't know how close he'd come to one hell of a surprise as the man swung his arm past his gun and to the satchel hanging from his shoulder. The bag was strapped diagonally across his torso so the satchel hung just behind his gun.

The young man brought his arm up to show Clint the envelope he'd removed from the satchel. "Are you Oliver?"

At the least, Clint had been expecting the kid to spout off some tough talk about how he thought he could take down the Gunsmith. At the most, he'd been expecting to get a shot fired at him. When he heard that question, Clint's only response was, "Huh?"

"Is your name Oliver?" the young man asked.

"No."

"Dammit. I was told this person was here playing cards." Suddenly, the young man turned his envelope around so he could get a look at it for himself. He then slapped it against his knee, sending a cloud of dust into the air from the dirty paper. When he looked at the envelope again, he rolled his eyes. "It's Olivia. I don't suppose that's either one of you?"

Rick let out a bellowing laugh. "Don't you ever look at what you're delivering, boy?"

"I'm not supposed to look at things too closely." With an embarrassed shrug, the young man added, "I just go where I'm supposed to go and drop off what I need to drop off. This is only my third ride."

Still eyeing the gun at the young man's side, Clint said, "Olivia stepped out for a bit. You can leave what you need to deliver right here."

"Are you her kin? I'm only supposed to leave something with—"

"Yeah," Clint said before the young man could rattle off too many objections. "I'm her cousin."

"Kissing cousin is more like it," Hartman muttered.

But the young man just seemed relieved to have heard Clint's answer. "Just be sure she gets this, all right?"

"Of course," Clint said in his most convincing tone.

The young man handed over the envelope so quickly that Clint wondered if he'd even needed to say he was her cousin.

"Thanks, mister," the young man said with a quick tip of his hat. He then turned and headed out the door.

"Good thing you weren't out to steal that," Hartman said.

"Yeah. It sure makes me think twice about sending anything through the mail again."

"Why?" Olivia asked as she walked into the saloon. "Are you afraid someone might say they're your cousin so they can steal your letters?"

"How long were you standing there?" Clint asked.

Walking up to the bar, Olivia replied, "Long enough. Now hand that over."

Clint had reached out to hand the envelope to her when he heard a gunshot from the street. "Good God," he said as he rushed to the window.

Rick hurried from behind the bar so he could get a look through the front window. Olivia was beside him, but stayed closer to Clint since he was armed with the Colt while Hartman had grabbed an old piece of lumber that had been chipped and dented on the heads of dozens of rowdy drunks who'd tried their luck against the saloon's owner.

Although it went against his better judgment to stick his head out where there had just been gunfire, Clint took a look through the doorway. The front window kept him from seeing too far in the direction from which the shot had come, but once he got a look through the doorway, he could make out the shapes of two men close to forty paces away from the saloon.

Smoke still hung in the air around the men's heads. Their arms were extended toward the saloon and their feet were planted in typical shooters' stances.

"Get back in here!" Clint said as he roughly pulled Olivia inside. He tossed her toward Hartman as he sighted down the barrel of his Colt and pulled the trigger.

More shots crackled through the air, but now one of the men outside at the corner was staggering back and sending his bullets straight over his own head.

Clint started to duck back into the saloon, but realized the young courier was still standing on the boardwalk. Apparently, the man was rooted to his spot and too petrified to even draw the gun at his hip. Since Clint didn't have much time to talk sense to the guy, he took hold of the young man's arm and nearly pulled it from its socket as he jerked him through the door.

As lead hissed past him and drilled through the front

wall of Rick's Place, Clint dropped to one knee and squeezed his trigger a few more times. His own shots must have been getting close to the mark because the two men at the comer were running for cover.

One of the men didn't make it.

Clint couldn't be certain if one of his later shots had hit the man or if his first one had finally dropped him, but the man dropped all the same. At first, it looked as if the man had simply lost his balance. Then, he fell over onto his side and hit without even trying to break his fall. Once he landed, the man didn't move.

"Damn," Clint said as he fired his last round at the remaining man at the corner. "I need to reload."

Clint felt a solid pat on his shoulder and heard a familiar voice from behind.

"I've got you covered, Clint," Hartman said.

Clint trusted the big Texan more than enough to take him at his word. Without looking over his shoulder to check, Clint jumped back into the saloon and emptied the spent casings from his Colt's cylinder.

When he looked over to check on the courier, he saw the young man's empty eyes just before he started to fall over. Clint might have been quick enough to catch the young man, but he was too late to save him. The bullet wound in the courier's back had already done its dirty work. As gently as he could, Clint lowered the young man to the floor.

Rick Hartman could have filled most of the doorway, but he only leaned out enough to bring his shotgun to his shoulder and take aim. The man who was still on his feet was too far away to be threatened by the shotgun, but Rick aimed higher and pulled his triggers anyway. The roar of the shotgun blasted like a cannon down the street, and Hartman stepped inside to dump the empty shells.

"That sent him running," Rick said with a smirk.

"Where'd he go?" Clint asked.

"He rounded that corner like a jackrabbit with his tail on fire. The other one's still laying in the street."

"Keep an eye on her," Clint said as he pointed to Olivia. "I'll be right back."

Without another word, Clint bolted through the front door and ran down the street. When Olivia started to go after him, she was stopped in her tracks when Hartman took hold of her arm. Tightening his grip just enough to keep her from moving, Hartman eased her back inside.

"We're staying right here, just like he asked," Hartman said.

"And what about him?" Olivia asked.

"He'll be back soon. He always is."

FIVE

Clint ran down the street with his gun drawn. It wasn't the most subtle way of getting from one spot to another, but it sure got the locals out of his way. The few people who weren't already ducking from the sound of the gunshots practically ran for the hills when they saw Clint coming.

Once he got to the spot where the body was lying on its side, Clint ducked down low and placed one hand on the fallen man's shoulder. He didn't want to be surprised if the man was just hurt and waiting for a clear shot, so he kept him within arm's length.

There was no trace of the one who'd gotten away. Clint kept his Colt ready to fire as he turned in all directions to search for any sign of where the man went. Although he couldn't see a trace of that fellow, Clint did spot a young boy wearing short pants crouched behind a water trough.

When the boy saw Clint looking at him, he pointed a small finger toward a nearby alley.

Trusting the kid on a gut level, Clint ran toward the alley. He made it there just quickly enough to catch sight of the gunman at the other end of the alley. Before Clint could fire a shot, the gunman whipped around and fired three of his own.

Clint used his momentum to rush past the mouth of the alley and slam his shoulders against the wall beside it. Once the gunfire had died down, Clint leaned out to get a look down the alley. All he saw was a brief flicker of motion as the gunman bolted away and to the left.

Before he took off after the gunman, Clint took a quick look at the water trough. Sure enough, the little boy was still behind it and was peeking around the trough at him.

"Thanks," Clint said.

The kid smiled and pulled his head back into safety.

Rather than run down the alley, Clint stuck to his end of the street and ran in the same direction the gunman had gone. Hoping the gunman hadn't taken too many unseen turns, Clint thought he might catch sight of him once he reached an empty lot between two stores.

Not only did Clint get the glimpse he was after, but he was almost trampled by the fleeing gunman.

Having taken a shortcut through the same lot, the gunman looked at Clint with wide eyes and swung at him out of pure reflex. If the gunman had only swung his fist, Clint might have leaned back enough to dodge the blow altogether. As it was, the pistol in the gunman's fist cracked against Clint's cheek and snapped his head to one side.

Clint let out a surprised yelp and scrambled to maintain his balance. The blow hadn't been enough to knock him out, but it stunned him in between steps so that his legs tangled up beneath him. He reached out to catch himself, and didn't quite fall. The pain was still making itself known throughout his head when he regained his balance and raised his gun.

The gunman was already off and running again. This time, he was headed for a horse tethered to a nearby post along the street.

As if he could feel Clint's sights on him, the gunman turned and pulled his trigger wildly. One shot after another erupted from his pistol. Hot lead whipped through the air, and a few shots even got close to drawing Clint's blood.

Rather than run toward the incoming rounds, Clint dropped in the dirt and fired a shot or two of his own.

Fueled by desperation, the gunman climbed halfway into his saddle and got his horse moving down the street. The horse had to have been a bit spooked as well, because it launched into a full gallop without much encouragement from its rider.

As Clint tried to take proper aim, one of the gunman's bullets thumped into the dirt near his left boot. The impact caused Clint to take a small hop away to the side, which also threw off his aim as he was pulling his trigger. The Colt bucked against his palm, but only succeeded in getting the gunman's horse to run faster.

Even though he knew what would happen if he pulled his trigger again, Clint took aim and did it anyway. Just as he'd figured, the hammer slapped against the back of a spent round. That loud metallic click might as well have been a slap on Clint's face.

"Damn it!" he growled as he fought back the urge to throw his pistol at the gunman's back.

As he reloaded, Clint hoped the gunman would turn around and try to make another run at him.

Unfortunately, the man wasn't that stupid.

SIX

The gunman lying in the street was dead. His eyes were open, but he didn't see any of the curious locals who inched forward to get a look at him. He also didn't see the grave digger lift him into the back of his cart and haul him away. Clint actually felt envious that the man didn't have to watch the commotion that followed or hear the questions posed by the law.

Clint stood there and did his part to help the law, but quickly felt like he could have been doing something more useful. The questions were done soon enough, and Clint made his way back to Rick's Place.

"That was fast," Hartman pointed out.

Clint looked around the saloon to find the place only slightly busier than when he'd left. "Didn't anyone come by to ask you what happened?"

"Sure. A deputy came and left. Seems like there's no shortage of folks with the same story to tell. Maybe next time you should keep your gun battles off the street."

"Very funny. Where's Olivia?"

"She's washing up." Stepping around the bar and a bit closer to Clint, Rick lowered his voice and added, "That kid who brought the letter didn't die until after you ran out of here. She seemed a bit rattled."

"Yeah. I know how she feels."

"Want a drink?"

Despite all the grief they gave each other, Clint and Rick had shared plenty of hard times. In fact, Rick Hartman was one of the few men around that Clint could take at face value. It was comforting to be able to talk with the man and not have to watch what he said or worry about what was actually going on in the Texan's mind.

"Yeah," Clint replied gratefully.

"One beer coming right up." As he headed toward the bar again, Hartman slapped Clint good-naturedly on the shoulder. "I'll just add it to the price of patching up my wall."

Clint sat down and rubbed his forehead. "Just add it to my bill."

"After all the windows, chairs, tables, doors, and walls that have been damaged throughout all the times you've traded lead with someone, you could probably have already bought this place out from under me."

"Actually, I think I could get a place a lot nicer than this."

Hartman walked over to Clint's table and set a beer down in front of him. "Fuck you," he said with a smirk.

Clint took a sip of beer and savored the familiar taste. When he looked up, he saw Olivia stepping through a door that led to one of the back rooms. Before she could take two steps through the door, Clint had rushed over to her side.

"How are you?" he asked. "Did you get hit?"

"You mean did I get shot?" she asked in disbelief. "Those two could barely seem to hit the saloon."

Clint couldn't help but be a little surprised by the easy tone in her voice, and that must have shown on his face.

"What's the matter?" she asked. "Did you think I'd be too shaken to walk?"

"Well . . . sort of."

Patting Clint on the arm, Olivia smiled and said, "I'm

feeling all right, but it could have been a lot worse if you hadn't been there. Thanks for getting me off that street."

"Don't mention it."

Seeing Clint's eyes drift toward the spot where the courier had been lying, Olivia said, "Someone came to take him away. He looked so young. Do you know who he was?"

"Not as such. All I know is that he came to deliver that letter." Suddenly, Clint straightened up and started patting his pockets. "The letter! In all the ruckus, I don't even remember if I . . ." He trailed off when he saw Olivia reach into the pocket of her skirt and retrieve something.

"You mean this letter?" she asked as she showed him the folded envelope.

"Good. You've got it. Do you know who it's from?"

"Actually," she said with a weary laugh, "things have been a little busy lately with the shooting and all."

"It's a good thing the law didn't take that from you," Clint said. "Did they ask about it when they were here?"

Now it was Olivia's turn to laugh. "They were here. Of course, they left well before you got back, so they didn't have a chance to do much more than ask where the shots had come from and where you went. The deputy seemed more interested in who shot first instead of why any shots were fired at all."

"Usually, that's the most important question they need to answer."

"Not this time. I would have told them more, but I thought it might be better to just wait for you to come back."

"So you didn't open that?" Clint asked as he pointed to the envelope.

"Not yet." Although she started tugging at the corner of the envelope, Olivia stopped before opening it. She looked at Clint and asked, "Do you think those gunmen were here about this?"

"I don't know. Let's take a look and see what's in there."

Olivia looked around as she slowly opened the envelope.

Her fingers went through the necessary motions as her eyes darted from one spot to another. She glanced at the window and door where she'd been when the shots had been fired. She looked at a few of the fresh bullet holes in the wall, and then wound up staring at the spot where the young courier had died.

When she finally did get the envelope open, Olivia removed a single piece of paper that had been folded in half. She unfolded the paper and only needed a few seconds to read what was printed there. Clint waited for her to finish.

As soon as Olivia looked up from the paper, he asked, "What is it?"

"My uncle," she said quietly. "He's dead."

SEVEN

"Your uncle?" Clint asked. "That's what was in the letter?"

Olivia nodded. "My Uncle Abner. I haven't heard from him in years."

Although he felt awkward questioning her about a dead relative, Clint had to ask, "Then . . . how did he know where to find you?"

"Come to think of it," Olivia replied as she examined the letter more carefully and then started looking at the envelope, "that's a very good question." After a few seconds and a lot of squinting, she held out the envelope for Clint to see. "Here you go."

Clint tried finding what had caught her eye, but too much dirt and a few water streaks made the printing on the envelope difficult to read. He took it from her and stared at it. "It's addressed to you via someone named Jenny in Dallas. Is that your aunt's name?"

"No. She's been gone for a while. Jenny's a cousin," she explained. "I was going to visit her while I was in town for the tournament."

"And she knew you were here?"

Olivia nodded. "I sent her a telegram so she wouldn't worry."

"Well, that explains a bit of it. There's still the question of how someone knew you'd be in Dallas."

"That's no mystery," Olivia said with a dismissive wave. "I told everyone I knew I'd be going to that tournament." Suddenly, she pulled in a quick breath. "Do you think someone's already gotten to Jenny?"

Clint let out a tired breath as he and Olivia walked back to his table. After pulling out a chair for Olivia, Clint settled onto his own and took a drink of beer. "The more I think about it, the more I wonder if those gunmen even cared whether you or I were there or not."

"What do you mean?" Olivia asked. "I was out on that street. I could have been killed if you hadn't pulled me back in here!"

"Yeah," Clint said patiently. "Those gunmen took a shot at that courier. After that, they shot at the saloon, but that could have been because I was shooting back at them. I think some others were shooting at them as well. They could have just been spooked."

Olivia placed her hands flat on the table and stared Clint right in the eye. She held her gaze for a few long seconds before asking, "Are you defending those killers?"

Placing his hands on hers, Clint stared right back at her without even blinking. "I sure as hell am not defending those men. In case you hadn't heard, I gunned one of them down myself."

Flinching a bit at the sound of that, Olivia started to nod. It wasn't long before she couldn't seem to look at him any longer. "I know you did. God, Clint, I'm so sorry I even—"

"Stop right there," Clint interrupted. "No apologies necessary. It's been a hell of a day."

He let out a breath and patted her hands once more before asking, "Would you like something to drink?"

"Desperately."

Clint got up and walked over to the bar. Rick Hartman

hadn't taken a step toward Clint's table, but was eager for Clint to get over to him.

"How is she?" Hartman asked as soon as Clint was at the bar. "She was shaking like a leaf before she asked to splash some water on her face."

"She'll be fine. Can you fix her up a drink? I didn't even ask what she wanted."

"Something to calm her nerves?"

"Yeah."

Nodding once, Rick said, "I know just the thing." As he gathered up some ingredients as well as a mug to hold them, Rick said, "You find out what was in that envelope? It must've been something pretty good to stir all this up."

"Not really. It was some bad news, but nothing that seemed bad enough to kill the messenger."

Hartman's head snapped up from what he was doing and he cracked a smile. "Hmm. Killing the messenger, huh? I didn't even realize."

After a second or two, both Clint and Rick shared a small laugh. Before too long, Hartman raised the mug he'd prepared for Olivia and said, "Here's to the messenger. It's just too bad he can't tell you anything that might be of any help. For that matter, even that gunman you dropped might have been of some use. It's a shame you're such a good shot."

Clint blinked and backed away from the bar. Suddenly, the tired smile he'd been wearing took on some more steam. "You're a smart man, Rick. You know that?"

"Yeah. What'd I do this time?"

"I'll let you know when I get back," Clint replied as he headed for the door.

Rick shrugged and walked around the bar to bring Olivia her drink.

EIGHT

A town the size of Labyrinth saw its fair share of trouble, but normally not enough to warrant regular hours to be maintained by the undertaker. The only reason Clint knew where the place was located was because he put Eclipse up in the same stable as the horses that pulled the town's hearse.

As Clint walked down the street toward the undertaker's parlor, it was late enough that most of the stores along the way were locked up for the night. This time, however, he was fairly certain that someone would be at the parlor. In fact, his modified Colt had made certain that the undertaker had something to keep him busy.

The front window had a dark curtain drawn over it. A sign in the door told him the place was closed and that he should leave a note if any services needed to be planned. But the dim light behind the curtain told Clint the place wasn't exactly empty.

"Hello?" he said as he knocked on the door. "Could you open the door?"

There was no answer.

He knocked again and waited, but didn't hear so much as a footstep coming from within the parlor.

Clint leaned over to the window and peered through the

narrow crack between the windowpane and the curtain. He couldn't see much, but he could see something moving in the back of the building. It looked like a large, open room, so Clint rapped his knuckles against the window.

That made a lot more noise as the knocking combined with the rattle of the glass within the pane.

"Excuse me," Clint said to the glass. "I need to have a word with you. It's important." When he saw a bit of movement, Clint added, "It's about the shooting."

He still couldn't hear footsteps, but Clint could see a figure approach the front door. Rather than try to stare through the narrow crack, he stepped over to the door and waited as someone fidgeted with the latch.

The man who opened the door had a round face and a few days' worth of stubble sprouting from his chin. "You're not one of the deputies."

"No. My na—" was all Clint got out before the door started to close. He was just quick enough to get his boot in the door and finish his sentence. "My name's Clint Adams."

The man seemed annoyed that Clint had kept the door open, but that expression quickly left his face. "Oh, I've heard of you. You own Rick's Place."

"No, but I'm a friend of his."

"Whose?"

Clint blinked as he tried to decide if the man was serious. When he came to the unfortunate conclusion that he was, Clint said. "Rick Hartman. He owns Rick's Place and I'm his friend."

Slowly, the man nodded. "Oh, yeah. I've heard of you."

"Can I come in?"

"We're closed."

"It's important. Like I said before, it's about the shooting."

"Right. What about it?"

"Those men were shooting at me," Clint explained. "They were also shooting at a woman and I was hoping to see if I could find out who they were."

"I've just got the two bodies here. I was about to get a coffin put together for each of them."

"And I won't get in the way," Clint quickly said. "Do you think I could get a look at what they were carrying in their pockets and such?"

The man narrowed his eyes and studied Clint carefully. "Did the sheriff ask you to come down here?"

No matter how easily Clint thought he could lie to the sleepy-eyed man, he shook his head. "The sheriff didn't ask me. I'm the man who did some of the shooting and I thought I'd look into it myself."

For a moment, it was unclear as to whether or not the man had heard Clint. Then, he stepped back so he could open the door and allow Clint to walk inside. As Clint moved past him, the man said, "Sometimes it's best to take care of things for yourself. More folks should do that."

"Yeah," Clint said earnestly. "They should."

"I'm George Lindenwood," the man said. He was a stout fellow with an ample stomach that hung a little bit over his belt. His hair was a bit too long and a bit too mussed. He also kept his mouth open a bit and made every breath a noisy affair.

"I really appreciate this, George. I'll try not to get in the way."

"You shouldn't be in my way because you won't be here long. Fact is, I don't know what you expect me to do for you. My job isn't much more'n digging holes and nailing coffins together."

"Where are the men's belongings?" Clint asked.

George became still again, but Clint was growing accustomed to that. As George thought things through, the only noise he made was his constant, gasping breathing. "They didn't have any valuables," he finally told Clint.

"I'm not out for valuables and I'm not out to steal anything," Clint assured him. "All I'm looking for is something that might tell me why they were here or why they opened fire. If you like, you can watch everything I do."

George stared at Clint silently for a few seconds before turning around and heading toward a back room. The parlor would have been completely dark, if not for a few lanterns burning in that adjacent room. The leftover glow from the lanterns seeped into the main room like water through a cracked barrel, casting wavering shadows from several ominous shapes.

While he wasn't exactly the sort to get rattled so easily, Clint found himself reflexively lowering his hand toward his gun as he made his way past several coffins that were propped up at various angles. The room was the sort of thing that scary campfire stories were made of, and the kid inside any man wouldn't have any trouble seeing ghosts in those corners.

"There's not a lot of room back here," George said as he moved through the small doorway.

As soon as Clint stepped inside, he knew that George wasn't kidding. The room was filled with tables and piles of lumber. The stench of death was almost thick enough to choke on thanks to the two bodies stretched out on what had once been bunk beds. The mattresses had been stripped off the wooden frames, leaving what looked like large shelves against the wall.

Clint didn't recognize the bodies at first, but that was mostly because they were stripped down and covered by white sheets as if they were tucked in for the night. Their bodies were perfectly straight and their heads were aligned so their eyes stared straight up into oblivion.

"Their things are in those boxes next to their feet," George explained. "Take a look through them if you like, but let me know before you take anything."

"Sure," Clint said.

The two boxes were right where George had promised,

and they'd probably held hats before holding the posses-
sions of dead men. The first box only contained dirty clothes
and a satchel full of letters and small bundles. There was
also a list of names with locations scribbled next to them.
The courier's pistol was at the bottom of the box.

The second box held more dirty clothes, two guns, and
a pouch of tobacco. When Clint searched through the shirt
and pants pockets, he only found one thing. Fortunately, it
was just the sort of thing he was after.

"Mind if I take this?" Clint asked.

George looked at the small item in Clint's hand and
asked, "That's it?"

"Yep."

"Sure," George said with a shrug.

Clint moved past the squat man and headed for the
door. Before he could make it very far, he heard George's
voice.

"You killed that one there?" George asked.

When Clint looked over at him, he saw the squat man
pointing at the courier stretched out upon the bottom bunk.
"No," Clint replied.

"Hell of a good shot either way."

"I suppose. You look busy, so I'll see myself out."

George nodded as he walked over to the boxes and took
a quick look through them for himself. He seemed satisfied
when he glanced back to Clint.

"When you're done with your work here, stop by Rick's
Place," Clint told him. "The owner's a friend of mine and
I'm sure he wouldn't mind buying you a drink or two for
helping me out."

George grinned and nodded enthusiastically. It wasn't a
pretty sight.

NINE

"Damn," Rick said as Clint walked into the saloon. "Don't you ever get to sleep?"

"Why?" Clint asked. "What time is it?"

"Time for me to close up and for any respectable man to turn in for the night."

"Well, I gave up being respectable a long time ago. Also, I sort of lost track of the time."

"That's fine," Rick said. "I thought you might need a reminder. That's the only reason I haven't locked up already. Where've you been anyway?"

"At the funeral parlor."

"Christ, you sure know how to spend your nights."

Now that Hartman had mentioned the late hour, Clint could barely keep his eyes open. It seemed the entire day had rushed upon him at once and now he had to pay the price. "Did Olivia leave?" Clint asked.

"A few minutes ago. I damn near had to carry her out of here."

"You do mix a potent drink."

Hartman smirked and replied, "That may have had something to do with it. I made her second drink a bit stronger since she seemed all fired up to wait for you. I know better than to assume you'll be back at a reasonable hour."

"I wasn't gone that long," Clint said in his own defense. "Anyway, I'm going to bed."

"Did you find anything at the funeral parlor?"

"Yeah."

"Are you going to tell me what it is?"

Clint stopped and then removed the small item from his pocket. Holding it out at arm's length, Clint said, "There it is."

"What the hell is it?" Hartman asked.

"A note that was in the dead gunman's pocket. It's got Olivia's name and a few locations on it. There's an address in Dallas as well as the names of a few saloons around here."

"Mine's on there?"

"Yep."

Hartman puffed out his chest and beamed proudly. "Seems like word's finally spreading about my saloon."

"Yeah. A few more shootings and a couple big poker games should put you right on the map."

"You're always good for plenty of both," Rick replied without missing a beat.

Clint couldn't come up with a good response to that. Rather than try to toss another barbed comment back at the Texan, he took another look at the note for himself. "These spots are places that have been holding some pretty good games lately. Any gambler looking to make a name for himself would want to pay them a visit."

"Or make a name for herself," Hartman pointed out.

"Exactly. My guess is that those gunmen were definitely out looking for Olivia."

"Then why shoot the messenger?" Rick asked.

Clint shrugged and tucked the small piece of paper into his pocket. "The kid didn't know when to duck. That's gotten plenty of folks killed."

"I suppose." Hartman's eyes narrowed as he studied Clint. "Why don't you get some sleep? Before you know it, you'll be wanting to ride off somewhere and you won't let up until you're falling from the saddle."

"Sounds like a good idea." Clint headed for the stairs that led up to the few rooms available for rent in the saloon. "See you in the morning." Before he got to the top of the stairs, Clint stopped and said, "Oh, by the way, I promised a few free drinks for the undertaker."

"You mean that fat fellow?"

"That's him. He was really helpful."

"I'm sure he was. He just . . . gives me the creeps."

Hartman watched Clint go up the stairs and head for his room, and made certain he was gone before he did anything else. Once he was sure, Hartman stepped out through the front door and walked down the street. He retraced the path Clint had taken moments ago, and quickly found himself at the funeral parlor.

After a few knocks, the squat man with the slack jaw answered the door.

"Hey there," Hartman said. "There's one last thing my friend Clint Adams forgot about."

"I've got work to do."

"It won't take a moment." When he saw no reaction from the other man, Hartman added, "It's worth a bottle of whiskey."

TEN

The next morning, Clint went over to Olivia's hotel for breakfast. When he arrived, he found her sitting at a small table by herself with most of her meal still in front of her. Although she seemed surprised at first, that expression quickly gave way to a smile.

"Clint! Come on over and join me," she said. "Would you like some eggs?"

"That sounds great."

She pushed her plate toward him and then smiled again.

The leftovers of her meal weren't exactly what he'd had in mind, but the food was still warm and he was about to pick up her fork when the plate was pulled away from him.

"I swear, men are animals," she said. "I was only kidding. Order what you like and it'll go on my bill."

Clint shrugged, and asked the old woman who served the food for the same thing Olivia had ordered. Once the old waitress shuffled off, Clint turned to Olivia and asked, "How'd you sleep?"

"Not bad."

"You seem to be taking the news about your uncle pretty well."

"Yes," she replied softly. "We weren't that close, but I always enjoyed visiting him."

"Do you know of any . . ."

Seeing him struggle with what he wanted to say, Olivia rubbed his hand and told him, "Go ahead and ask. Losing that bet last night has brought us a bit closer, you know."

Clint couldn't help but smirk at the memory of losing the bet. He wore a more serious expression when he asked, "Do you know of anything your uncle might have been involved in?"

"Like what?"

"I don't know. Just anything out of the ordinary or that could have turned out badly."

Slowly, Olivia started to nod. "You mean anything that could end up with a couple gunmen trying to shoot me?"

"Yeah. Something like that."

"No. Those gunmen might not have known anything about me or my uncle, though." Stabbing some eggs with her fork, she added, "For all we know, they could have been shooting at you. I imagine a man like you is used to things like that happening."

Despite the edge in Olivia's voice, Clint took her words with a grain of salt. He reached into his pocket, took out the piece of paper, and asked, "Where were you planning on staying when in Dallas?"

"Excuse me?"

"Was it the Alhambra?"

Olivia looked stunned. "Yes. How did you know?"

"The real question is how the person who wrote this knew." With that, Clint showed her the piece of paper.

"What is that?" she asked.

"I found this in the pocket of a dead man."

After snatching the paper from Clint's hand, Olivia read it over. "This has my name on it. There's also the name of just about every place I was planning on going to."

"One of the men who shot at us yesterday was carrying that. I know you just heard about your uncle and I know you don't want to think badly about him, but those gunmen weren't just firing at us by mistake. They were gunning for you or maybe that courier as well."

Slowly, Olivia shook her head. "No. They were after me. What else could it be? My name is the only one on this paper."

"Which brings me back to my other question."

Olivia handed back the paper and sipped her coffee. "I'm sorry I got cross with you. Part of me was already worried about the things you were just talking about, but I was hoping it wasn't true. Now that I know it's true, I wish . . . well . . . I just wish it wasn't."

"Yeah, I imagine it must be sort of odd. You've probably got plenty of good memories about your uncle, but those probably don't go along too well with what you're hearing now."

"Actually," Olivia said with a chuckle, "they fit in pretty well. He was always into something or other. Uncle Abner was the one who first taught me to play poker."

"Really?"

She nodded. "He used to teach me card games whenever he'd visit. Once I started getting better at them and we began playing for pennies, he wasn't invited to stop by so often. That was a long time ago."

"What about your cousin Jenny? She knew where you were. Maybe you should visit her for some answers."

"I couldn't," Olivia replied while shaking her head. "Not after what just happened."

"Why not?"

"It seems pretty dangerous. You may not believe this, but not everyone looks forward to getting shot at."

"I know I sure don't look forward to it."

"But you know how to live with it. Just thinking that there's someone else out there who might have my name written on another piece of paper like that sends a chill down my back."

"Then maybe you shouldn't go by yourself. Maybe," Clint added as he leaned back so the waitress could set his plate in front of him, "you should take along someone who is used to that sort of thing."

"I don't know anyone who'd be foolish enough to do something like that," Olivia said as she glanced knowingly toward Clint.

"Oh, don't try to pull any wool over my eyes," he grumbled as he scooped some eggs onto his fork. "You would've gotten me to take the job whether I'd wanted to or not."

"You don't have to do anything you don't want to." Placing her hand on his, Olivia said, "I mean it. There's already two men dead, so I don't want to put you in danger as well."

"Don't think anything of it. Besides, how can I expect to win our next wager unless I keep you good and close?"

ELEVEN

After breakfast, Clint returned to Rick's Place. He didn't see Hartman behind the bar, but that wasn't such a surprise considering how late Rick had stayed up the night before. Clint packed up his things and headed back down the stairs with his saddlebags over one shoulder. By the time he reached the bottom of the stairs, Clint saw Hartman stepping out from one of the supply rooms.

"There you are," Rick said. "Sleeping late, I see."

"For your information, I've already washed up and had breakfast."

"Where are you taking those bags?"

"Over to the stable and then across Eclipse's back. After that, I'll be taking them to Dallas."

"Good. You might also be interested in this." Hartman held up a satchel and then tossed it across the room.

Clint reached out with one hand and caught the satchel by its strap. Holding it up for a closer look, Clint spotted some familiar markings. "This belonged to that courier."

"Actually, it belongs to whatever company he works for."

"Then I'm sure they'll send someone for it."

"Just take a look under that flap."

Setting the satchel on the closest unoccupied table,

Clint opened the flap and found a few letters and a delivery log. He flipped through it and found record of three letters addressed to O. McKay.

When he saw that name, Clint flipped through the log a second time. Looking up at Hartman, he asked, "Where'd you find this?"

"The funeral parlor."

"What made you think to look for it?"

"Just something you said about why someone would want to shoot that courier. It occurred to me that there was only one good reason to shoot a courier and that was for whatever he was carrying." Hartman crossed the room so he didn't have to shout. "Don't feel so bad, Clint. I'm sure you would've thought of it if you hadn't been so tired."

"So maybe that courier was killed on purpose?"

Hartman shrugged. "All I know is that if he wasn't, he was standing in the very worst spot at the very worst time. Hell, even that grave digger said it was a nice, clean shot."

"Yeah, he did." Clint balled up his fist and resisted the urge to punch a wall. "I should have taken this satchel when I was there."

"Hey, you can't think of everything. That's why they say two heads are better than one."

"Did you go through the rest of these letters?" Clint asked.

"Yeah, but I didn't find anything too interesting. You can just drop them off at the company whose mark is on the satchel."

"You mean I'm supposed to deliver these?"

"Of course," Hartman replied with a somewhat shocked expression upon his face. "The mail's gotta be delivered or else the whole system falls apart."

Clint shook his head, closed up the satchel, and slipped it over his head, even though he secretly had no intention of getting sidetracked by delivering mail. "Any other chores for me to do?"

"Yeah. Next time you need to pay someone off for a favor, don't give away my whiskey."

"Take the price of that grave digger's drinks out of what I won off you in poker. That's probably the only way I'll get you to repay me for it anyway."

"Especially since you cheat like the devil."

Shaking his head, Clint walked toward the door. "Thanks for the beer and backup," he said.

"You just be sure and watch yourself, Clint. Things have a nasty habit of turning nasty when you get involved. If you'd like someone to watch your back, I wouldn't mind a quick ride to Dallas."

Clint stopped at the front door and turned around to find the big Texan standing with his arms crossed sternly over his chest. "I appreciate the offer, Rick, but you've already watched my back plenty. This could just be nothing more than a family dispute."

"Look me straight in the eye and tell me you believe that."

Clint looked Hartman in the eye, paused, and then tipped his hat. Without anything more than that, Clint left Rick's Place.

TWELVE

A couple hours later, Clint and Olivia had left Labyrinth and were headed for Amarillo. The open country of West Texas was spread out before them like a multicolored quilt. Overhead, the sky stretched out in all directions with only the stray white cloud to mar the field of blue. Even though they were bound for the train station in Amarillo, seeing the smoke from a steam engine headed in the same direction was more like seeing a dirty smudge upon a fresh painting.

"Maybe we should just ride to Dallas," Olivia said.

Clint looked over at her and the tan mare she rode. "That's a fine-looking animal you have, but I doubt it can outrun a train."

"I'll bet yours could."

"Maybe, but not all the way to Dallas. Don't you want to get there as quickly as we can?"

"Yes," Olivia said anxiously. "Just the thought of sitting on a train for . . . who knows how long . . . just seems like torture."

"The way you've been squirming, you could probably run to Dallas faster than that train."

"I bet I could!"

"Really?" Clint replied. "Care to make a wager about that?"

Olivia looked over at him and smiled. She held her reins in a loose, comfortable grip and her hips shifted perfectly to match the movements of her horse. With Eclipse staying directly beside her, Olivia and Clint might as well have been strolling along a boardwalk.

"What kind of wager?" she asked.

"Since you're feeling like running so fast, why don't we have ourselves a race?"

"You want me to race you to Dallas?"

"How about to those telegraph wires?" Clint replied.

Looking at the trail ahead, Olivia picked out the line of posts that carried the wires in a path that crossed directly in front of them somewhere between half a mile and three quarters of a mile ahead. "All right," she said. "What's the wager?"

"Same as before?"

She shook her head. "I already won that one. How about something interesting?"

"That was pretty interesting to me."

Although Olivia put on the appearance of thinking it over, she actually didn't have to think very long before she snapped her fingers and said, "You're right. But let's say you have to show me something new."

"You mean, if you win."

"Sure."

"And what if I win?" Clint asked.

"Then you can have some more of what interested you so much the last time."

Clint shook his head. "Nope."

"What?"

"You heard me. If you want to bump up the stakes for me, then yours should go up as well."

"All right," she said with a pout. "What did you have in mind?"

"Simple," Clint replied. "If I win, you'll tell me something I don't know about you."

Olivia studied the trail leading to the telegraph lines. "All right," she said reluctantly. "If that's the way you want to play it. Then, go!" And with that, she snapped her reins while tapping her heels against the sides of her mare.

Even though Clint had been expecting something along those lines, the speed with which Olivia had given herself a head start was a bit of a shock. What surprised him even more was just how much steam the tan mare had in her stride.

Clint knew Eclipse well enough to know the Darley Arabian was anxious to get moving. Just seeing the mare bolt and feeling the thunder of hooves through the ground was enough to cause all of the stallion's muscles to tense.

Although he gave the reins a flick, Clint held back from allowing Eclipse to hit full speed. Even at the somewhat subdued pace, the stallion was doing a fine job of catching up to Olivia. And then, once he could feel Eclipse was taut as a bowstring, Clint touched his heels to the Darley Arabian's sides.

He might as well have pulled a trigger because Eclipse took off like a shot.

Leaning forward in the saddle, Clint held onto the reins tightly and adjusted to Eclipse's movements. Since the ground was flat and open, there wasn't even a need for him to steer.

It was the best kind of riding there was. As Eclipse gained speed, Clint forgot about everything else that was happening in the world around him. There wasn't room for him to worry about anything but staying upright and not stopping.

Soon, Clint didn't even feel like he was in the saddle. Instead, it felt more like he was falling forward and there was nothing to be done about it but keep riding.

Olivia's mare put up a good fight, which meant it took slightly longer than Clint had anticipated to catch up to her.

Once he drew up alongside Olivia, Clint looked over and gave her a wave. One more snap of the reins meant the race was over.

The telegraph lines were still about a quarter of a mile away.

THIRTEEN

The train pulled out of Amarillo on schedule. It let out its screaming whistle and once the pistons got moving, the entire metal beast started to roll and smoke billowed out from the stacks.

"I still say you cheated," Olivia said as she looked out the window to see the platform disappear from sight.

Clint laughed and settled onto the uncomfortable bench toward the back of their car. "How could I have cheated?"

"I don't know, but you would have found a way."

"This is coming from the woman who was sharpening her skills at palming cards just a couple days ago."

"Was it only a couple days?" she asked. "Feels like it's been weeks. I wonder if there's any food being served on this train."

"Don't go wandering off," Clint told her. "Just stay put and get some rest."

Olivia scowled at him and pulled away as if he'd grabbed her arm. "I'll go where I please, thank you very much."

"That other gunman got away, remember? I don't know where he might have gone."

"I think we would have noticed if he'd been following us."

Clint was about to dispute that, but couldn't do so with a straight face. The trail to Amarillo had been wide open and most of it had been covered at a fast gallop. Even if someone had been trying to track them, they wouldn't have caught up before Clint and Olivia had boarded the train.

"Either way," he said, "we should be on the safe side."

"Then why don't you accompany me to the dining car? That is, if there is one."

Clint started to protest, but wasn't able to get out one word of wisdom before Olivia was up and heading toward the narrow door leading out of the car. Rather than put up a fuss, Clint got up and followed her to the next car.

He was getting hungry anyway.

There was a dining car, but it had more tables and chairs than actual food. When Clint sat back down at the little square table where Olivia was seated, he felt like he was stepping into the den of a starving animal.

She eyed him intently and asked, "What did you find out?"

"Well, I found out that we should be able to eat when we reach Abilene."

"That's your good news?"

"Abilene's our next stop," Clint offered. "That's pretty good news."

Olivia crossed her arms, leaned against the window, and didn't move from that spot until the Abilene station rolled into view.

Strictly speaking, taking the train was faster than riding to Dallas on horseback. When it came down to all the sitting and waiting in discomfort while choking down sandwiches made with stale bread, the trip seemed a whole lot longer. At the moment, however, Olivia seemed happy as a clam.

Savoring her second ham sandwich, Olivia smiled to herself and reached for her cup of water. The dining car was still mostly empty, but she sat at her battered little table as if she were in a fine restaurant. When she looked around for one of the porters who was acting as a waiter, she instead spotted a lanky man with thick stubble on his face glaring at her from the connecting door.

Instinctively turning away from the man, Olivia settled behind her table and looked around the car. There were only three other occupied tables, and two of them were being used to host makeshift card games. When she heard the knock of heels against the floor, she wished the table was something a little more solid than some chipped planks partially nailed down to keep them in place.

The train's whistle shrieked through the air, but wasn't loud enough to mask the sound of the approaching steps.

Olivia patted one of her skirt's pockets to find the derringer still in its place. The little gun wasn't much comfort, however, when she thought about the hungry fire that had been in the man's eyes.

She didn't want to look behind her.

Olivia didn't need to turn around to know the man was there. She could hear his steps and could practically feel the heat coming from his body. The only thing that frightened her more was when those steps came to a stop directly behind her.

As the sound of the train's whistle faded away, Olivia could hear the subtle rattle of the connecting door opening again. Since she'd been focusing on that noise, the sound of the voice coming from less than a foot behind her made Olivia jump.

"Surprised to see me, sweet thing?" The voice hissed.

Olivia still didn't want to turn around. Instead, her eyes frantically darted about for any indication that anyone else in the car was taking notice. The men at two of the tables were absorbed in their games, and the woman at the third table was feeding her child as if there was nobody else around.

Olivia's hand inched toward her derringer as a second set of footsteps approached her from behind.

"I know you saw me." The voice snarled. "Truth is, I was just as—"

Suddenly, Olivia heard a loud slap followed by the scuffle of boots against the floor. She, along with everyone else in the car, turned around to get a look at what was going on. Unlike everyone else in the car, however, Olivia smiled when she saw the lanky man being hauled toward the connecting door.

"Why don't we take this outside?" Clint said as he dragged the lanky man toward the door by the scruff of his neck. "These folks are trying to eat."

FOURTEEN

"You see?" Clint said as he dragged the man from the dining car and tossed him onto the small iron balcony between cars. "This is what I get for stepping outside for a few minutes."

The lanky man was close to Clint's height, but was wiry and wriggled like a snake as he tried to shake free of Clint's grasp. His clothes were dirty rags and his hat only seemed to be held together by thick layers of trail dust. Even the stubble on his face looked more like growth sprouting from the desert floor than anything coming from a living thing.

"You got the wrong man, mister," the lanky man said.

"Really? Then why were you hanging over that woman like some kind of buzzard?"

"Maybe I made a mistake, too."

Clint laughed and said, "I saw you reaching for that gun at your side. That sure as hell was a mistake."

The man's lips were curled up into a sneer and his eyes darted down toward his holster. Even though Clint was standing too close for him to get a look at his pistol, the man seemed to gain some confidence from knowing the gun was there.

With a sudden burst of movement, the man leaned back and brought one knee up. Clint was just quick enough to twist so his hip caught the brunt of that knee instead of his groin. Even so, the impact was close enough to send a cold wave of pain through Clint's lower body.

The lanky man was still moving. When he brought his knee back down, he stomped his heel on Clint's foot. Clint wasn't quick enough to avoid getting hit that time, and he felt the crunch of his foot being ground under the man's boot.

Rather than let the pain take too much of a hold on him, Clint used it to stoke his own fire. He tightened his grip on the man's collar, balled up his other fist, and then pulled the man closer while delivering a short punch to his gut.

The lanky man let out a pained wheeze and crumpled around Clint's fist. He then leaned forward a bit until the top of his head pressed against Clint's chest. From there, the lanky man snapped his head upward and caught Clint squarely on the jaw.

Clint had no way to see that coming. One moment, he was preparing to end the fight, and the next moment, he was blinded by a blunt pain in his jaw. When he tried to take a breath, the pain became so intense that it robbed him of the breath that was already inside his lungs. Clint's next impulse was to get the hell away from the lanky man so he could regain his senses without getting knocked out.

Blinking furiously, Clint cleared his head just in time to see the lanky man coming at him. Instead of taking another swing at him, the lanky man lowered his shoulder and ran straight at Clint. This time, Clint was able to tense his muscles in preparation for the impact.

The man's shoulder didn't hurt Clint, but felt more like a dull thump. While he was still feeling that jarring impact, Clint also felt himself being shoved backward. He staggered past the connecting doors of the cars. Before he could think about how close he was to the railing behind him, Clint felt his legs and backside slam against the iron bars.

Not wasting any time once he had Clint off balance, the lanky man sent a series of short, chopping punches to Clint's ribs.

Clint gritted his teeth and got a look at the man's face. He could see the joy in those eyes as the man landed one punch after another. Now that he had a good idea of where to aim, Clint leaned back to give himself enough room to deliver a punch of his own. His arm snapped straight up, glanced along the lanky man's chest, and sent his knuckles into the man's throat.

The punches to Clint's ribs stopped.

The lanky man clasped both hands to his throat and let out a hacking cough.

His eyes were wide open, and somehow managed to stay on Clint no matter how hard it got for him to draw a breath.

Clint stepped away from the railing and touched the spot on his face that hurt the most. There was a trickle of blood from the corner of his mouth, but nothing much worse than that.

For a moment, both men just stood motionless and looked at each other.

Then, the lanky man's hand drifted down toward his gun.

Although the lanky man made a fairly quick reach for his weapon, Clint was even quicker. But Clint didn't reach for his own gun. Instead, Clint reached out to grab the gun from the lanky man's holster, and managed to take possession of it less than a second before the man could get a grip around the handle.

Clint pulled the gun up and out of the lanky man's fingers. He then kept his arm moving as he chucked the pistol over his shoulder so it could sail completely over the railing.

"There," Clint said. "What are you going to do now?"

The lanky man answered that question by turning toward the door of the next car and pulling at the handle.

"Oh, no, you don't," Clint snarled as he lunged forward to pull the lanky man back in much the same way he'd pulled him from the dining car.

Instead of fighting Clint the way he had before, the lanky man reversed his steps while twisting at the waist. Clint tried to lean back, but still got clipped by the man's elbow as it swung past his face. There wasn't much behind that elbow, but the impact turned Clint's head and sent him stumbling away from the door. Since the lanky man was still in Clint's grasp, he came along for the ride as well.

Just as Clint righted himself, the man caught his foot on the grate of the balcony under his boots. If the lanky man had been hard to wrangle before, that task became almost impossible once he was stumbling awkwardly with all his weight behind him.

"Hold on," Clint said as he felt himself being pulled toward the railing. "What the hell are you doing?"

If the lanky man had an answer to that, he wasn't able to give it. He was too busy tripping over his own feet and finally tumbling over the rail. He hit the railing with his hip, completely lost his balance, and pitched over the side.

Using the same speed he'd used to snatch the man's gun from its holster, Clint grabbed hold of the man's other arm. He was barely able to get a grip on him, however, since the lanky man was flailing in a blind panic.

Wind whipped past Clint's face. The train's wheels clattered against the tracks. If the man let out a yelp or cried out, his voice was washed away by the train's sounds so Clint couldn't even hear the man. Of course, Clint had other matters on his mind, like leaning halfway over the rail and trying not to fall from the train headfirst.

"Hold on!" Clint shouted as dust and rocks pelted his face and the wind sent his hat flying away.

The lanky man's face was twisted into a mask of fear. His mouth hung open and his eyes were wide, despite all the grit being blown at him.

Clint tried to get a better grip, but only felt his fingers closing on empty sleeves. The man's arms were bony and slipped too easily from his grasp.

"You've got to hold on to me!" Clint shouted. "Otherwise, you're gonna fall!"

But the lanky man already seemed to be considering that option. He twisted his head around to get a look at the ground passing less than a couple feet or so under his dangling boots. Some clumps of weeds and grass were almost tall enough to whip against his ankles.

"Lift your leg onto that rail!" Clint instructed. Even as he spoke those words, Clint wondered if the man could hear a single one of them. The sound of his own voice was barely making it to Clint's ears through the rest of the train's noise.

When the man slipped another inch or two down, Clint leaned forward and clawed his way toward the man's elbow. Already, the weight of the man was close to pulling Clint over the side. After that last little slip, Clint could feel the impact of the man's boots knocking against the side of the train or possibly even the ground.

Clint pulled up with one hand and grabbed hold of the man's arm with his other hand to pull the man up as if he was pulling a thick length of rope.

And then, before Clint could do anything about it, the man was gone.

Because Clint had been pulling so hard, he staggered back from the railing as soon as the lanky man's weight was no longer dragging him down. Clint ran back to the rail and leaned over to get a look for himself. He saw the man rolling away from the train amid a thick clump of weeds.

Just then, the door to the dining car opened and Olivia stuck her head outside.

"Have you been standing out here the whole time?" she asked.

FIFTEEN

When the train arrived in Dallas, Olivia was the first one off. Not only had she been anxious to leave the train since the moment she'd boarded it, but she'd also gotten more and more nervous as Clint told her what had happened with the lanky man who'd snuck up on her.

"You're sure nobody is following us?" she asked as she hurried away from the platform.

Clint walked beside her and struggled to keep up. "I saw the man rolling in the grass, remember? Even if he could run after the train, I doubt he was too anxious to try."

"Well, there could have been another one somewhere, you know."

When Clint reached out to grab her hand, Olivia turned as if she was going to take a panicked swing at him. "What are you doing?" she snapped. "We're here. Let's get away from this train."

"You want to give your horse up to the railroad? I know I don't."

Olivia stopped and let out a frustrated breath. "Fine, but if either one of them are waiting for us, then it's your fault."

Leading the way back to the platform, Clint wrapped his arm around hers as a gentle way to make certain she

didn't get away. Once he got a look at where they were un-
loading the animals from the livestock car, Clint turned her
in that direction.

"So," he said calmly. "You saw more than one of those
men?"

Looking over at him, Olivia was quick to reply, "Did
you see another man? You only mentioned one."

"But you made it sound like there were more of them."

"I only saw one. Actually, I barely even saw him."

"You sounded pretty sure of yourself," Clint said. "In
fact, I think you may have let it slip more than once."

Olivia narrowed her eyes as if she were mentally sifting
through every last thing she'd said since she'd first stuck
her head out that connecting door. Finally, she rolled her
eyes and let out a breath. "There may be more than one of
them."

"How many?"

"Just one other."

"So you know them?" Clint asked.

Suddenly, Olivia's frown disappeared and she began
pulling Clint toward the ramp where the horses were being
led from the train. "Look! There she is now," Olivia said,
referring to her mare.

Olivia tried to walk away as if she were simply strolling
through a field of daisies, but Clint tightened his grip
around her arm just enough to hold her back. When she
turned to show him a surprised set of wide eyes, he wasn't
having any of it.

"Who are they?" he asked. The tone in his voice was
more than enough to convince Olivia to be quick about a
response.

"I thought I recognized the one in the dining car," she
explained. "I could have been wrong."

Clint scowled at her without saying a word.

"All right," she said. "I did recognize him once I saw
you dragging him out on his heels."

"And how come you didn't mention that until now? I believe it was still a pretty good bit of a ride between then and here."

"Did I mention how wonderful it was that you dragged him away like that?" she asked innocently. "I must say, it made me feel—"

"Like being quiet and eating another sandwich?" Clint asked. "Yeah. I noticed that much."

Since the horse tenders were looking for someone to claim Olivia's tan mare, Clint led her over toward the ramp. Once she claimed the horse as her own, Olivia turned to Clint and said, "I've known the Nagle brothers since I was small. I guess when I saw what happened, it took me a little while to figure out what to do."

"Great," Clint sighed. "I was already feeling badly enough for dropping that fellow off a moving train. Now I find out he was a childhood friend of yours."

Olivia laughed a few times and shook her head. "I said I knew the Nagle brothers. I sure wasn't friendly with them. They were always rotten little jackasses and the last time I saw them, they were rotten big jackasses."

Keeping his eyes on the slow procession of horses being led from the train, Clint asked, "You saw two of them on that train?"

"Not exactly. It's just that I never knew Boris or Wilson to draw a breath unless they were close enough to see the other one doing it."

"Boris and Wilson Nagle, huh? Which one did I meet?"

"That would have been Boris."

The more he thought about it, the more Clint felt the knot in his stomach tighten. "Shit," he muttered. "For all I know, he was sneaking up on you to ask what you've been doing since the last time you met."

"No, Clint. He wasn't."

"Are you sure? What did he say to you?"

"It's not what he said. It's . . ." She sighed and took the

reins that were finally handed over to her by the young handler. After smiling and paying the railroad worker, Olivia rubbed her horse's nose and said, "The last time I saw Boris Nagle, he was about to force himself on me."

Clint chewed on the inside of his cheek and nodded. "All right. I don't feel bad about him anymore."

"And you shouldn't. I think you also saved my life, because he swore to kill me the next time he saw me."

"He was out to kill you?"

Olivia nodded. "The last time I saw him, he was about to force himself upon me, but he didn't get too far. When he tried to grab me, I beat the tar out of him with a shovel and turned his balls into mush with my heel. What's so funny?"

Smirking and holding back his laughter, Clint held up his hands. "Did he do any more than just grab at you?"

"No! He wanted to do more. He told me so! What's so goddamned funny?"

"Nothing, it's just that pitching him off a train seems kind of light by comparison. I'm not laughing at you, Olivia. You just took me by surprise is all. I've heard of grown men putting up less of a fight when they're cornered."

The defensive scowl slowly faded from Olivia's face. Soon, she cracked a smile of her own. "Boris always had some lewd comment or other for me, and then he started bragging about what he'd do if he got me alone. That time, we were alone and he made a move. I stood up for myself before he could get the chance he was after."

"And you saw to it that he wouldn't be much use to a woman after that day, by the sound of it."

Now, Olivia did start to laugh. "He stopped saying lewd things to me for a good, long while. Of course, that's when his brother Wilson threatened to kill me."

"What?"

She nodded. "Boris may be a piece of horse shit, but I could handle him before he did much of anything. Wilson, on the other hand, scares the living hell out of me."

Clint believed her when she told him that. In fact, he hadn't seen that much fear in her eyes when the lead had been flying in Labyrinth.

"If Boris was here, Wilson can't be far away," Olivia said. "And he won't be too happy when he finds out what happened to his brother."

SIXTEEN

Boris Nagle rode into Dallas on a horse, covered in blood. His clothes were tattered and filthier than normal, but his eyes were burning with enough rage to divert any comments that folks might have wanted to make when they saw him.

He didn't even bother going to the train station. It was well past dark and the train from Amarillo had already been loaded up and sent on its way a long time ago. Instead, Boris rode to Thompson's Varieties on the corner of Market and Main Streets.

Once he was in the saloon district, folks stopped glancing at him twice for looking like he'd been thrown off a train. In fact, Boris wasn't even the most raggedy person in sight. Some of the drunks littering the street looked more like animals than human beings. Boris kicked one of the sleeping old drunks out of his way as he walked into the crowded saloon.

Boris had barely made it through the front door before he was pulled aside by a tall man with angular features and a narrow frame wrapped up in taut layers of muscle. Boris started to fight back, but stopped that real quickly when he saw who it was who had practically snatched him off the street.

"Wil?" Boris said as he squinted at the lean face that stared directly at him. "I nearly—"

"Save it," Wilson Nagle growled. "And shut your mouth."

Boris still had his arm cocked back to throw a punch, but eased it down as he looked around cautiously. "Is someone watching us?"

Wilson had already turned his back and was walking toward a table situated against the wall. Although the saloon was full of people in various states of drunkenness, Wilson walked through them as if they weren't even there. The ones who didn't step aside were shoved aside and forgotten. None of them was anxious to do much more than toss a few mumbled insults at Wilson's back.

When he arrived at the table, Wilson stopped and glared down at the man sitting there. "You're in my seat."

The man looked up at Wilson and didn't seem impressed by the tall, slender figure in front of him. "It was empty when I got here, so it's mine now."

Without another word, Wilson took the mug from the man's hand, dumped it on his head, and smacked him across his face with it so hard that the man toppled from his chair and hit the floor. Wilson sat down and motioned for Boris to take the other chair.

"Hey!" the man hollered.

Wilson stood up, picked up his chair, and then slammed the legs down onto the man's back. After dropping the man to his belly, Wilson set his chair down so one of the legs was resting on the back of the man's hand and then sat back down again.

The man let out a pained scream that lasted until Wilson placed his heel on the man's head and ground his face into the floor like he was putting out a cigarette.

"Take a seat," Wilson said with a cordial wave of his hand.

A few of the others at the nearby tables gave Wilson

some shocked glances, but Boris wasn't surprised. He just shook his head and sat down.

"So why all the urgency?" Boris asked. "Does someone know you're here?"

"I don't know," Wilson replied. "I was just sick of waiting for you. Why the hell weren't you on that train?"

"Because I fell off it, that's why!"

Wilson nodded and said, "I guess that's why you look like shit smeared on a shingle."

Glancing at the people at the nearby tables who had already been examining him and his brother, Boris leaned forward and lowered his voice. "Olivia McKay was on that train and . . . what's so funny?"

When Wilson grinned, it was almost a frightening sight. His pointed chin, narrow cheekbones, and long nose made him look more like a ghoul than a man. When he started to laugh, he didn't make a sound. "Isn't she the one who beat you down with a shovel?" he asked.

Reluctantly, Boris said, "Yeah."

"And then she pounded you in the—"

"Yes! I said that's her, all right?"

Wilson nodded and forced himself to stop laughing. The smile faded a bit, but still lingered like a stain upon soiled sheets. Rocking a bit on his chair, he listened to the sounds of the man screaming on the floor. When the man tried to get up, Wilson slammed his boot against the top of the man's head. "So she threw you off the train?"

"No. She didn't throw me anywhere. She had some other fellow with her."

"Who was it?"

"I don't know," Boris snapped. "But I almost killed him. He just got lucky when I tripped over the rail."

"That's pretty damn lucky," Wilson pointed out. "How is it they even wound up on the same train as you? Weren't you supposed to do your business in Labyrinth and then come back as soon as you could? Weren't you supposed to ride back instead of on some train?"

Boris pulled open the front of his shirt so the top two buttons came loose. That way, his brother could see the blood-soaked bandages looped around his shoulder. "There's more just like 'em around my ribs. Things went to hell real quick with that courier and I nearly got killed along the way. I wasn't in no condition to ride back here, so I headed for Amarillo and caught the train there. At least I was able to get a message to you."

"Yeah," Wilson scoffed. "But I didn't need no telegram to tell me my brother's a goddamn woman who can't handle a simple job or the ride after it's done."

"Look, I wound up on that train and got a closer look at that son of a bitch who tried to shoot me. He's probably just some gunfighter that Olivia hired to protect her when she got that letter."

Wilson's eyes narrowed as he leaned forward. The man under his chair grunted, but stayed in his place without putting up too much more of a fuss. "She wasn't supposed to get that letter, Boris."

"I know."

"You told me you had some friends that would see to it that that letter wound up burned. You promised."

"I know what I promised. I followed that damn courier through West Texas, but his damn horse was fast enough to keep ahead of me."

Shaking his head and sifting his finger through long, knotted hair, Wilson said, "All couriers have fast horses. That's why they're couriers."

"I caught up with him and Olivia in Labyrinth, shot the courier dead, but was almost killed by that asshole who threw me off the train."

"He was in Labyrinth with Olivia?"

"Yeah," Boris said.

"So he is staying close to her," Wilson mused. "Which means he'll be here as well."

"At least we know where Olivia will be headed now that she's here."

"Do you know this man's name?"

Boris shook his head once. "No. I barely got a look at him in Labyrinth since he was shooting at us and all."

"And on the train?" Wilson asked.

Grinding his teeth together, Boris let out an angry breath and shook his head again. "We didn't exactly get to introduce ourselves before he was dragging me away from Olivia."

"And what were you doing with Olivia? Are you still sweet on that bitch?"

Boris jumped up and started to lunge across the table at his brother. Wilson merely watched and grinned when Boris backed down before laying a finger on him.

"I see you still are," Wilson said. "That ain't good. If we're to get our hands on that inheritance, you gotta be able to cut that shit loose."

After sitting back down again, Boris forced a smile onto his face. "I did get some things done on that train before it all went sour. I gave that gunfighter's horse a little present."

"And how the hell do you know it was his horse?"

"I saw him loading it onto the train when him and Olivia got on."

"You always did have a good eye for horses, brother."

"Yeah. I can make 'em run or I can make 'em gimp. This horse won't be running too much farther once he starts walking around a bit."

Wilson nodded. "That is good news. And I am glad to have the chance to meet this hired gun myself. Come on," he said as he got up. "We've got a social call to make."

The man under Wilson's chair stayed down until he was certain both brothers were gone.

SEVENTEEN

Eclipse was one of the only things Clint could always count on. Apart from a handful of people scattered throughout the world, that horse was one of the only living creatures that Clint could trust with his life. At the moment, however, he wasn't so willing to be so forgiving.

"Jesus," Clint grunted as he tightened his grip on the reins and tried to hold Eclipse back without hurting him. "You really didn't like being cooped up on that train!"

The Darley Arabian waggled his head and snuffed angrily. So far, he had yet to stand still for more than a second. His hooves scraped or stomped against the dirt and he fought to pull the reins from Clint's hand. It was one of the first times since Clint had first laid eyes on the stallion that he was reluctant to climb into the saddle.

"He probably just wants to be ridden," Olivia pointed out. "Maybe you should stretch his legs a bit."

"Sure, and maybe you'd like to take your chances?"

As soon as Clint asked that question, Eclipse reared up a bit and churned his front legs in the air before dropping down again.

"What is wrong with you, boy?" Clint asked.

"It couldn't have been anything in that train car," Olivia said. "Zel's fine."

Clint looked over at her and then looked at the tan mare Olivia was leading down the street. The mare simply blinked back at him as if to make herself an even bigger contrast to the fit Eclipse was throwing. "What kind of name is that for a horse anyway?" Clint grunted.

Olivia almost started in on that story, but was cut short by another angry whinny from Eclipse. She hopped to the side a bit and said, "There's something wrong with him and it's more than just being anxious from the train ride."

"Yeah," Clint replied as he pulled on the reins and tried to calm the stallion down.

"Do you think he's hurt?"

"I think he's not his normal self, that's for sure. Just help me get him somewhere safe so I can figure out the rest."

"What do you want me to do?" she asked cautiously.

Eclipse's eyes were frantic and every time his front hooves touched the ground, his entire front half sprang back up again. Each time that happened, he pumped his legs more violently than the last.

Wrapping the reins around one hand, Clint tightened his grip around the leather as he reached out to place his other hand on Eclipse's neck. "Just keep clear and make sure nobody gets in front of us," he said. Once Eclipse snapped a hind leg out in a quick kick, he added, "Or behind us."

"I don't think that's going to be a problem," Olivia said as she took a look around.

There were plenty of other people along the street and on either side, but none of them seemed interested in coming within a mile of the bucking Darley Arabian. In fact, most of them looked as if they were trying to get as far away as possible.

"Do you know where I can take him?" Clint asked. "A stable or blacksmith or anyplace will do, just so long as it's close."

"There's a stable down on Lamar. It's close to a man who really knows his way around—"

"Sounds great," Clint said as he struggled to keep Eclipse from bucking any more. "Lead the way."

Clint let Olivia get ahead of him a ways before pulling on Eclipse's reins. The Darley Arabian responded instinctively, but was still very agitated. As they moved slowly down the street, Clint patted Eclipse's neck and spoke soothingly to him. Although he didn't expect the stallion to understand any of the words, Clint could tell his voice was calming Eclipse down. At the very least, the stallion had something else to focus on instead of whatever was causing him to fret so much.

Before Clint rounded the next corner, he already had a good idea of what was causing Eclipse to throw such a fit. Fortunately, Olivia didn't waste any time in bringing him to a small blacksmith's shop connected to a narrow stable that was just big enough to hold two horses.

"Whoa, there!" a burly man with a pudgy, clean-shaven face hollered. He wore a thick cotton shirt with the sleeves rolled up and a heavy apron marking him as a blacksmith.

"Do you own this place?" Clint asked.

"Sure I do, but there's a stable right across the street."

"My horse doesn't need a stable. Right now, he needs to get something taken out of his hoof."

All the blacksmith had to do was watch Eclipse take a few steps before he waved toward one of the empty stalls. "Take him in there, but you'll be the one to keep him still while I have a look."

"I doubt it'd work any other way."

EIGHTEEN

The blacksmith's name was Ross Emmory. He was a sturdy fellow with no fear of death, and was perfectly willing to put his well-being on the line for his chosen profession. Clint learned that much by watching Ross wade into the flurry of Eclipse's legs, which were being thrashed about like so many branches in a windstorm. Unlike those branches, however, getting hit by one of these could put a man down for good.

Ross kept his head low as he waited for Clint to get a handle on Eclipse. At the first sign of an opening, Ross dove in to grab hold of Eclipse's front right leg. It was a hell of a struggle, but the blacksmith and Clint eventually calmed the stallion down enough for Ross to get a look.

"Yep," Ross grunted as he wrapped an arm around Eclipse's leg. "There's something in there all right."

Clint had an arm wrapped around Eclipse's neck and his other on the saddle horn. That way, he could wrangle the Darley Arabian well enough to keep him from getting any ideas of making a run for it. "Hold on another second," Clint said. "It feels like he's calming down."

"I sure ain't about to let go."

Both men held on as Eclipse ran out of steam. Actually,

Clint could see the stallion's eyes well enough to know there was plenty of steam left inside Eclipse's heaving frame. The Darley Arabian was simply returning to his usual self.

"Keep that leg up," Clint said. "It seems to be doing the trick."

"I'll bet it is," Ross replied. "I can already see there's something jammed up under his shoe."

"What is it?"

"Can't say just yet, but it doesn't look like something that was just trampled on by mistake."

Within the next few seconds, Eclipse settled down so he just let out a few snuffing breaths every now and then. Soon, he situated himself on three legs and held his foreleg up on his own. Once Eclipse was in that position, Clint could feel the stallion's muscles loosen as a relieved breath came from all three of them.

"There now," Ross said. "Let's have a look."

The blacksmith kept Eclipse's leg in one hand as he reached for what looked to be a small milking stool. He settled onto the stool and then reached for one of the tools hanging nearby.

"Need any help?" Clint asked.

"Just keep that boy steady. That's what I need from you."

"No problem," Clint replied as he rubbed Eclipse's ear.

Ross shook his head and let out a wary chuckle. "Don't get too relaxed just yet. That boy's got some fire in his belly. I'm about to find out why, so hang on tight."

Keeping his hand on Eclipse's head, Clint tightened his grip on the saddle horn.

After letting out a slow breath, the blacksmith got to work prying off Eclipse's shoe. The Darley Arabian squirmed a bit, but seemed even more relieved once the shoe was off.

"There's your problem," Ross said.

Clint leaned to try and get a look without letting go of Eclipse or the saddle. "What's the problem?"

"There's a tack wedged up in a soft spot here. Could also be a nail."

"What?"

"Yep," Ross grunted. "I'll let you know in a second." From there, the blacksmith worked and pulled like a dentist trying to yank a stubborn tooth. Eclipse let out a few uncomfortable grunts of his own, but stayed fairly still. Finally, Ross leaned back and held up a nail that was bent at something close to a ninety-degree angle.

"There it is," Ross said. "I daresay either one of us would be pretty rowdy if we had this thing stuck in our foot."

"What is it?" Clint asked.

"Looks like a nail that was chipped in half. It could also be a hobbler."

"A hobbler?"

"Yeah," Ross said with disgust. "Someone places this just right and the poor animal won't even know he's got something in his shoe until he takes a few steps. The more he takes, the farther in it gets. The real trick is in placing them so they can't be seen right away, but still do their damage. It takes a special sort of asshole to do this on purpose."

"Sure does," Clint said. "And I think I might know who had a hand in this."

"Well, give him a punch in the mouth for me."

"It'll be my pleasure."

NINETEEN

Olivia was waiting outside for Clint when he left the blacksmith's shop. She rushed over to him the minute she spotted him. "Is he going to be all right?" she asked.

"It wasn't anything life threatening," Clint said with a forced smile. "Just something stuck in his shoe."

"Thank God."

"By the looks of it, someone put a hurting on Eclipse on purpose. Do you think one of your old acquaintances might have been inclined to do something like that?"

Olivia didn't even have to think that one over. Nodding slowly, she replied, "Boris Nagle was always good with horses. He could break wild mustangs and was even better at stealing them."

"Have you ever heard of a hobbler?"

Once again, Olivia nodded. "Boris made those as a joke. He used one on my horse when he thought he would try to make his move on me. I suppose he didn't want me getting away so easily."

"Then he sounds like the man I'm after. Maybe once Eclipse is feeling better, we can ride out and see if he's laying hurt somewhere along those tracks."

"How long will it be before you can ride again?"

"Ross said it shouldn't take long and I believe him. Eclipse seemed better the moment that thing was taken out from under his shoe."

"Good. Would you like to come along with me to Jenny's?" she asked. "Maybe it'll take your mind off that poor horse."

Clint waved toward the blacksmith's shop and said, "Eclipse may have been hurting, but I can tell Ross has a soft spot for horses. I think Eclipse'll be spoiled rotten after just a few nights over there. We did come here to take care of this business, though, so let's get to it."

Olivia led Clint through Dallas to a stretch of homes that looked to be fairly new. As she guided him down the street, Olivia told Clint about a series of fires that had raged through the Dallas area some time ago. Apparently, some sections of town were quicker to rebuild than others. Whatever the reason for it, the homes Clint saw were easy on the eyes and well maintained.

Just as Olivia picked out one house in particular and headed for the door, a woman with short brown hair rushed outside while waving her arms excitedly. "Olivia! You came! I'm so happy to see you!" the woman shouted.

Olivia opened her arms and ran to meet the woman. Once they collided, both of them hugged and jumped while chattering anxiously. Still walking slowly toward the house, Clint stopped when he saw the shorter woman set her eyes on him.

"Who's this?" the woman asked.

Olivia smiled and said, "This is Clint Adams. He came along with me from Labyrinth."

Before Clint could get a word out by way of an introduction, he saw the short woman rushing toward him. She hadn't seemed very big when she'd been rushing at Olivia, but the woman seemed particularly solid when she charged at Clint.

Sure enough, Clint was nearly knocked off his feet by

the stout woman. In fact, she almost picked him up and swung him like a rag doll.

Trying to keep herself from laughing too hard at the panicked expression on Clint's face, Olivia said, "Clint, this is my cousin Jenny."

"Yeah," Clint gasped from within Jenny's locked arms. "I figured."

As soon as Jenny let Clint go, she was rushing back to her house. "Come inside, both of you," she said. "I just made some lemonade."

Her house was tidy but modest. Her lemonade was delicious and Jenny's smile was infectious. After the two women had done a bit of catching up, the conversation shifted to more pressing matters.

"I got your telegram telling me you'd be showing up," Jenny said. "Then I received a package. It's Abner's."

Olivia reached out to pat Jenny's hand. "I know," she said consolingly. "I heard about what happened to Uncle Abner."

"Do you know how he . . . how . . . ?"

Rather than let Jenny say the words she was obviously dreading, Olivia said, "No. All I know is that he passed."

"Frankly, I'm amazed anyone could track you down," Jenny said with a smile. "I know about all the wandering you've been doing as well as all the gambling."

Olivia nodded. "I know."

Jenny shrugged and grinned. "I've heard you've even done your share of winning. Good for you."

When Jenny smiled, Olivia seemed to be taken by surprise. Her cheeks flushed and she patted Jenny's hand some more. "Thank you." Turning to Clint, she asked, "See why I like her so much?"

Clint held up his glass and said, "She won me over with this lemonade."

"Family recipe," Jenny explained.

"What about the package you got?" Olivia asked. "Could you tell me what it is?"

"Actually, that package is why you're here. I'm supposed to give it to you along with another letter."

Jenny stood up, gathered the empty glasses, and headed out of the room. She returned a few seconds later, carrying a rectangular bundle roughly double the size of a brick.

Taking the package, Olivia held it up to her ear and shook it. "Do you know what it is?" she asked.

As Jenny sat down, she nodded and said, "I already told you what it was."

"You did?"

"Yes. It's Abner."

Olivia stopped shaking the package and lowered it from her ear. All the color had drained from her face.

TWENTY

Olivia was lying in one of Jenny's spare beds. The room was small, yet warmly decorated to make a guest feel every bit as welcome as a family member. There were doilies on every tabletop and a Bible lying next to the bed. None of these amenities seemed to make much difference, however, to the pale woman who lay stretched out on the bed.

For his part, Clint couldn't keep his eyes off the brick-shaped package lying on a nearby table. "Do you think that's really . . . ?"

"I don't know and I don't want to know," Olivia said.

"Come on, now. You must want to know . . . even a little."

Olivia's hands were pressed against her eyes as if she meant to push her head all the way through the pillow beneath her. Slowly, she moved her hands away and looked at Clint. She then looked at the bundle before glancing back at Clint. "Maybe," she whispered.

"You want me to open it?"

Sitting up quickly, Olivia gathered her legs up beneath her and leaned forward. "Yes."

Clint picked up the bundle and held it in his hands. It wasn't too heavy, but it didn't exactly feel solid. Instead, it felt more like dirt or sand had been clumped up and was being held together by the wrapping. Tugging slowly at the twine keeping the bundle shut, Clint looked at her and asked, "Are you sure?"

"Yes, now just open it. But be careful. I don't want you to spill it."

"Trust me, if this is what Jenny said it was, I don't want to spill it either."

The twine needed to be cut, but Clint had a pocketknife for that. He didn't cut the paper, however. Instead, he peeled it open carefully and made certain not to pull too much of it open too quickly. When he got one end open, Clint held it open to look inside.

"What is it?" Olivia asked.

"Looks like a pouch."

After pulling away the rest of the paper, Clint was left holding a thick burlap pouch. Unlike the original bundle, this package had no give to it. Whatever was inside the pouch filled it almost completely.

As Clint was trying to decide whether or not he wanted to open the pouch, Jenny knocked on the door. Since the door was already open, Clint and Olivia only had to look in that direction to find Jenny standing there with something else in her hands.

"When I found out what was in there," Jenny said as she nodded toward the pouch, "I had a word with the undertaker here in town. He wanted to see that pouch for himself on account of it being such an odd kind of burial, but I thought you should see it first. Anyway," she added while holding out her hands, "the undertaker gave me this. He said it's customary for occasions like this."

The thing in Jenny's hands was a clay pot that looked as if it had been sliced apart toward the top instead of having a proper lid. There wasn't much of a design on the pot, but it did look to be about the same size as the pouch in Clint's hands.

"It's made to hold Abner," Jenny explained awkwardly. "At least, what's left of him. Once he's inside, we can seal it up so it stays shut."

"Why would . . . why would he . . . do this?" Olivia asked. "I mean, why would Abner have this done? Was it his idea?"

"I don't know, sweetie," Jenny replied. "Maybe you should read the letter that came with it."

"You haven't read it yet?"

Jenny shook her head. "It's addressed to you." With that, she reached into the pocket of her apron and removed a piece of paper that looked to be folded into quarters. "Here," she said while handing the paper to Olivia.

"Thank you," Olivia said as she meekly accepted the paper. Turning it over in her hands, Olivia found the paper to be sealed on two sides by wax. It was a mess of smeared wax all over the paper, but it had gotten the job done.

Jenny started to leave, but stopped before taking more than a few steps away from the door. Slowly turning back around, she held her hands clasped in front of her and asked, "Do you think I could stay? I've been dying to know what's in that letter."

"Sure," Olivia said with a smile. "Abner wouldn't have wanted it any other way."

Jenny smiled and nodded before walking over to one of the chairs situated against the wall. Once seated, she folded her hands on her lap and waited patiently.

Using her fingernail to chip away at the wax, Olivia methodically worked her way around the paper until the seal had been broken and flecks of wax were covering the bed. She unfolded the paper, shook some more bits of wax away, and then started to read. It didn't take long for her face to shift through several different shades of emotion.

"What is it?" Jenny asked.

Clint wanted to know the same thing, but was content to sit and wait for Olivia to speak. Part of him even wanted to ease out of the room so he wasn't intruding on a personal moment between family members. Before he could start to make a move for the door, however, Clint saw Olivia look straight at him.

"Abner was murdered," she whispered.

"What?" Clint and Jenny asked at the same time.

Olivia nodded slowly. "It says right here that someone was after him. He came into some money and started getting threats." As she spoke, she flipped between two pages that comprised the letter.

"Someone came after him and he hid his money somewhere safe. The letter says he meant to tell where the money was before he died." Lowering the paper, Olivia asked, "Does it say anything about that in your letter, Jenny?"

Jenny shook her head solemnly. "Not a word. My letter just said to expect you and if you didn't come, that I was supposed to carry him to that river."

"What river?" Clint asked.

"It's in this last part," Olivia said as she turned over the second page. "Uncle Abner was always afraid of dark spots, so he didn't want to be buried. Instead, he wanted to be burned and then scattered along the Rio Grande where he grew up." Olivia lowered the papers and looked at Clint with tears running down her cheeks. "It was his dying wish."

TWENTY-ONE

"Who does something like this?" Olivia whispered a few hours later.

She and Clint had been treated to a hot meal followed by some of the best peach cobbler he'd ever tasted. Jenny had cooked the meal and offered a few consoling words, but seemed more than willing to let Olivia eat in peace. Although she gave Clint a stern look after dinner, she hadn't said much of anything when he followed Olivia to her room and shut the door.

"What do you mean?" Clint asked.

Olivia reached out to touch the bundle that was still wrapped in paper. "This," she said as if she was afraid of waking the dead. "I mean, is this even Christian?"

"There's nothing wrong with it," Clint told her. "It's not typical, but it's been done for a long time. I don't know exactly how he managed it, but I've heard of . . ." Pausing before he went into too much explanation of what little he knew regarding the process of turning someone into a pile of ashes, Clint said, "It can be done. Actually, I've seen Indian ceremonies along those lines and they're quite beautiful."

She looked up at him and asked, "Really?"

Clint nodded. "Haven't you ever heard of that before?"

"Not really. Most of my family lives to be old and cranky. I don't think I've ever even known someone who's died. Well, not until now."

"There's not much to say about it," Clint replied with a shrug. "It's bound to happen to all of us."

"Yes, but does everyone else have to carry someone's ashes all the way to a river?"

Clint tapped his chin as he pretended to think about it for triple the amount of time he needed. Finally, he shook his head. "Nope. I think that's pretty strange."

Olivia took those words exactly as they'd been intended and smiled. "That about sums up Abner. It's only fitting that he's buried the same way he lived. Well . . . deposited . . . or sunk. Whatever it is we're supposed to do with him."

"I believe scattered is the word you're looking for."

"Yes. That sums up Abner as well."

Even though Clint hadn't known the man, he had to laugh at that. "Sounds like he was a hell of a man."

"He sure was."

"Do you know any who'd want to hurt him?"

"No. That's what's been bothering me. I can't think of what would possess someone to come after Abner. Most folks either loved him or didn't even know him very well. I don't think he had any enemies."

"All it takes is one lucky strike," Clint pointed out. "You'd be surprised how quickly the enemies pile up after that. At least, we already know who was coming after him."

It took Olivia a moment, but she was soon able to snap her thoughts away from the bundle on the table. "Right! The Nagles."

"Would they have known if your uncle had come into any money?"

"Abner and the Nagles lived within a few miles of each other ever since he moved away from the Rio Grande. They didn't get along, but they were always in each other's business." Her eyes narrowed and her voice took on a distinct edge. "I could see Wilson Nagle pulling something like this."

"My guess is that your uncle wasn't foolish enough to make it well known if he came into money."

"It wouldn't matter. That piece of trash Boris always happened to be in the right place at the right time. If he doesn't hear things, he spies until he does hear something. He probably found out about my uncle's windfall."

"All right," Clint said. "The only thing we're missing is where that money is."

Olivia stood up and walked over to the table where the bundle was lying beside the clay jar. "I don't care where he got it or how much it was. All I want is to put Abner where he wanted to be."

After taking a breath to steel herself, Olivia took the top from the jar and emptied the bundle into it. For the most part, it sounded like sand being poured into the jar. Every so often, something would clatter against the clay.

She kept her hands against the top of the jar and tried not to think about what could be clattering among the ashes. She also tried not to pour quickly enough to send up a cloud of gritty dust.

Once the gruesome task was finished, she went to the window and clapped her hands outside. "There," she said quickly. "A little of him here is nice, right?"

"Yeah," Clint said. "Why don't I take that to get it sealed?"

"Thanks. I need to wash up."

TWENTY-TWO

Although he hadn't been too eager to visit another funeral parlor, Clint's trip to the one in Dallas was quiet and uneventful. The undertaker was a friendly old man who'd been the one to deliver the clay jar to Jenny in the first place. He'd also been the one to craft it with his own hands. Once Clint handed it to him, the old man wet the part of the jar where the two halves met and then smeared the clay together.

"There you go," the old man said as he carefully handed back the jar. "Just let it dry overnight. If the seal cracks, wet it some more."

"I think I can handle that," Clint replied. "Do I owe you anything?"

"Just take care of that urn and see to it that it gets where it needs to go."

"You know about this man's request?"

"No," the undertaker replied. "Most folks who take 'ashes to ashes' so literally usually intend on winding up somewhere other than a grave. If I may ask, where is he going?"

Clint had been around too long and had dealt with too many snakes like the Nagle brothers to leave any bread crumbs lying around. Rather than tell anyone where he was headed just so they could possibly tell someone else, Clint said, "The river."

That seemed to be enough for the old man, because he smiled and nodded solemnly. "A real good place. You takin' him there?"

Clint nodded. He then held up the urn and looked at it from all sides. "Will this stay together during a ride?"

"Long as you don't drop it. Even then, it should stand a good chance."

As Clint inspected the urn, he heard the rattling inside. Rather than ask the gruesome question that was rattling around inside him, he looked at the undertaker and held his eyes there until the older man grinned.

"Just bits of bone and such," the old man said in response to the unspoken question. "Probably some teeth or if he had any fake ones or fillings or the like. Not everything burns up and turns to ash, you know."

"Guess I just never really thought about it."

"Most folks don't. Have a good trip, mister. You're doing a kind thing by taking someone for their last ride. Whoever he was," the old man said as he reached out to pat the top of the urn, "he's surely grateful."

Clint left the parlor with the urn tucked under his arm. It wasn't a long walk to the blacksmith's shop and when he got there, he found Ross with a large set of tongs in his hand.

"Back already, huh?" the blacksmith asked.

"Just thought I'd check in on my horse. I hope he hasn't been much trouble."

Ross waved that off after he set down the tongs. "I've had a lot worse. By the way, I didn't get your name."

"Clint Adams."

Extending his hand, Ross waited until Clint shook it. As anyone might expect, the blacksmith's grip was tough and nearly strong enough to crack a few bones.

"That's a fine horse you got there," Ross said. "You must take real good care of him."

Clint nodded and replied, "I try."

"Well, there's plenty of folks who don't try nearly as hard. I just wanted to tell you that."

"Well, thanks."

"Now, on to the bad news. I got that hobbler out and there ain't no more in there, but you should let him have a few days of rest before you ride him anywhere."

Clint set the urn down and walked over to Eclipse's stall. The Darley Arabian was a completely different animal from the wild-eyed stallion he'd been before. Not only was Eclipse calmer, but he looked plain tired. "How much damage was done?" Clint asked.

"Luckily, you caught it quick," Ross told him. "But there's still a wound there and I'd hate to shoe him just yet. If you absolutely need to move him, I can nail around the spot that was . . . well . . . let me just show you."

When Ross walked over to Eclipse and immediately knelt down to the freshly bandaged front leg, Clint reflexively wanted to pull the man away. He knew Eclipse well enough to figure the stallion wasn't tired enough not to kick the head off anyone who poked around that sore hoof. But since the blacksmith seemed to be doing well so far, Clint let him go now.

"You see?" Ross asked as he lifted Eclipse's leg and peeled back some of the bandages.

To Clint's surprise, Eclipse merely blinked and shifted his weight. It was hard for Clint to doubt someone who'd gained the Darley Arabian's trust so completely. Looking down at what Ross was showing him, Clint could see a bloody crack in Eclipse's hoof.

"That looks like it hurt," Clint said.

"You're damn right it did," Ross told him. "I can make a shoe that can allow that to heal. I can nail the shoe on so it don't make anything worse. But there ain't nothing I can do if he bears a full load on his back and runs for miles on end. From what I've already seen of this boy, he won't say no to doing any of that if you're doing the asking. That means I'm asking you to ease up and don't push him too hard."

Clint rubbed Eclipse's neck and nodded to the blacksmith. "How long should it take before he can be back to normal?"

"A few weeks."

"All right. Make that new shoe and put it on. Think you can have it ready by tomorrow?"

"I was just about to start on it now," Ross said. "You in a rush to get out of here?"

"Yeah," Clint replied as he picked up the urn, "but we can afford to wait a little bit."

TWENTY-THREE

The next couple of days were quiet.

That, more than anything else, surprised Clint.

Olivia had spent some time with Jenny, catching up on old family rumors as well as swapping a few new ones. They reminisced about Abner and spoke a bit about what was to happen next. Whenever Olivia would spend too much time talking about that, Jenny would change the subject to something easier to handle. For the most part, Jenny understood, and she often eased everyone's spirits with some freshly baked dessert.

While all of this was going on, Clint looked out the windows almost as much as he looked over his shoulder.

It was another quiet, sunny day when Olivia walked up to stand beside Clint on Jenny's front porch.

"What's bothering you?" Olivia asked. "Is Eclipse doing better?"

"Yeah, he's doing fine."

"Then something else must be under your skin. You haven't stopped pacing for days."

"I don't know." Lowering his voice as he looked around again, Clint said, "After everything that happened when this trip started, I was expecting something else to happen by now."

Olivia smirked, crossed her arms, and stared out at the same patch of street that had captured Clint's attention. "You don't feel comfortable unless someone's shooting at you?"

"That's not it and you know it."

"Oh, then maybe it's been too long since you threw someone off a train?"

Clint wheeled around to look directly in her eyes as he replied, "I didn't throw anyone off a train! I tried to . . ." But then he saw the grin on Olivia's face, so Clint turned back around.

"Glad to see you've still got some spark in you," she said. "I haven't even been able to interest you in visiting my room the last few nights."

Lowering his eyes, Clint shot a quick glance back at the house. "Are you kidding me? I feel like I'd have to watch for every creaky floorboard and then glue my mouth shut for fear of making too much noise."

Olivia leaned over and whispered, "That could turn out to be fun, don't you think?"

"Sure. Only, you're not the one who might get knocked out by one of those rolling pins or pans I see hanging all over that kitchen of Jenny's. The women in your family have a tendency to be awfully hard on a man who steps out of line, remember?"

"Oh, don't be silly. Jenny likes you."

Clint smiled. "She looks after you like a mother. It's plenty clear that she wouldn't take kindly to any funny business going on under her roof."

"Has that ever stopped you with anyone else?" Olivia asked.

"Actually, no."

"You're still worried about one of those Nagles coming after me, aren't you?"

"Coming after you or Jenny," Clint said. "If there was just one of you to look after, things might be a bit easier. But those two know you, which means they probably know where to find Jenny. Boris was on that train, so he was on his way to Dallas anyway. Do you think the other one is far from here?"

Olivia shook her head and leaned against Clint. "Probably not."

"It's been a few days," Clint said. "If you're going to take the ashes to the Rio Grande, we should go soon. The longer we wait, the braver those brothers are going to get."

"Do you think Boris survived that fall?"

"Honestly, he might not have survived if I hadn't tried to keep him from falling. The more I think about it, the more foolish I feel."

"Why? Because you didn't let a man die?" Olivia rubbed Clint's shoulder and told him, "A guilty conscience is one thing, but you should never feel guilty for having a conscience."

"You know what would make me feel a whole lot better?" Clint asked.

"What?"

"If we could get a move on before either one of those Nagles decides to take a run at us."

"So you're sure you want to come along for the rest of this?" Olivia asked.

"Of course. I've already come this far."

"Good," she said with a little smirk. "Because I think I've finally found out where we're supposed to go."

Clint had to look at her for a few moments to see if she was joking. "I thought you said you knew where to go."

"I was there a few times when I was small, but I'm not certain about the exact spot."

"Well, that might be useful. It is a big river, you know."

When he got no reaction from Olivia, he added, "You don't know much Spanish, do you?"

She furrowed her brow and asked, "Why?"

"Never mind. What were you saying?"

Shaking her head as if she'd gotten some dust on the end of her nose, Olivia moved along. "I've been doing more than just swapping stories with Jenny. She had some of Abner's things that were sent along. I wanted to go through it so I could hopefully find something to jog my memory as to where exactly along the Rio Grande he grew up. I remember going there as a little girl, but that was a long time ago."

"Doesn't Jenny know anything about that?" Clint asked.

"Maybe, but I think she forgot as well. When I first started talking to her about it, she didn't seem to recall much. I figured it might be safer for her if she didn't know. That way, there's no reason for Boris or Wilson to bother her too much."

Clint knew a thing or two about the wickedness that went through a killer's head. Most killers didn't need a good reason when it came to inflicting pain. There was some logic to Olivia's intent, however, and Clint was reluctant to give her one more thing to worry about.

"I think the best thing we can do for her is get out of here before anything happens," Clint said.

"Right. And now that I've remembered where to go, we can get going. It shouldn't be too bad of a ride if we get started soon."

Wincing at the sound of that, Clint said, "I don't know if Eclipse is up for a long ride. What about the train? Is there one bound for wherever we're headed?"

"I doubt it, but there might be one that'll get us closer. I could always go on my own, though. It's been so quiet that—"

"You're not going on your own," Clint insisted. "Let's just see how close the railroad can get us and then we'll ride the rest of the way. Eclipse just needs to take it easy for a bit."

"Well, make sure he's good enough to start walking now," Olivia said. "He looked like he was in a lot of pain. I'll go check the train schedules."

"I'm coming with you," Clint insisted. "We've been careful this far. There's no need to let up now."

Olivia seemed annoyed by Clint's bullheadedness, but brightened up once she saw him offer her his arm. She slipped her arm around his and accompanied him to the train station.

TWENTY-FOUR

Olivia bought two tickets on a southbound train that was scheduled to leave the next morning. Since there were no trains that went to the exact spot where she needed to go, they could afford to be a lot less choosy when it came to picking their destination. Even though there were no rails that came within sight of Abner's childhood home, the train ride would shave a good portion off their journey.

The main thing was that Eclipse wouldn't be forced to spend too much time on his bad leg. Clint headed to the blacksmith's shop to check on Ross's progress. He also wanted to make sure it wouldn't do more harm than good to ride so soon.

When he stepped into the blacksmith's shop, Clint only saw Eclipse. There was no horse in the second stall and Ross was nowhere to be found. Rather than look around the place on his own, Clint tried to catch Ross's attention the old-fashioned way.

"Ross?" he shouted. "You in here?"

There was no response.

"Ross? It's Clint Adams."

"Hold on," Ross hollered from somewhere past the horse stalls. "I'll be right there."

Clint rubbed Eclipse's nose, and was glad to see the familiar sparkle in the Darley Arabian's eyes.

"I figured I'd find you here," someone said from the doorway.

Recognizing the voice right away, Clint turned and placed his hand on his Colt. "You've got a lot of nerve showing your face to me again, Boris," Clint said. "Maybe I should take that hobbler of yours and shove it somewhere so you'll know how it feels."

Boris Nagle grinned and nodded. "I wouldn't hurt no horse. He looks fine to me."

"Yeah. Why don't you come over here and see for yourself? Or are you moving a little slow as well?"

The grin dropped off Boris's face. "You tried to kill me, you son of a bitch."

"You were doing your fair share on that train, if you recall. Besides, you had to have stuck that hobbler in before I laid eyes on you."

"I suppose I did."

Clint nodded and resisted the urge to lunge at Boris right then and there. The simple fact that Boris hadn't moved from his spot or reached for his gun told Clint that he didn't want to make the first move.

"Tell me, Boris," Clint said. "Where's your bro—"

Clint's question was cut short as something heavy cracked against the back of his skull. The impact flooded Clint's head with dull pain as his ears filled up with the loud rush of blood. Soon, that rush was joined by the flow of air rushing past his face as he fell to the straw-covered floor.

Wilson stayed close to Clint, even when it meant crouching down over Clint's unconscious body. He still gripped the club he'd used to put Clint down. In fact, Wilson even raised the short length of polished wood as if he was about to start bludgeoning Clint some more.

"What the hell is going on here?" Ross asked as he emerged from a narrow door in the back wall.

Both Nagle brothers glared at Ross for a few seconds. Neither of them was in a position to convince anyone that they were simply there to pay the blacksmith a visit.

TWENTY-FIVE

It wasn't long before Ross spotted Clint sprawled on the floor. His thick, callused hands tightened around the new handle he'd gotten from the back room to replace the broken one still wedged into his hammer. "You get away from him," the blacksmith warned.

"If you know what's good for you," Wilson growled as he reached into Clint's pocket, "you'll go right back where you were and forget what you saw."

Ross thought that over for a second or two, which was the amount of time he needed to figure out which of the two brothers he should charge first. Since Wilson was closer and looked ready to cave Clint's skull in, Ross chose him.

The blacksmith took a long step forward as he swung the handle of his hammer. If the handle had been attached to the iron head, it would have killed Wilson right then and there. As it was, Wilson was able to lean back just enough to only get clipped by the end of the handle.

With the sound of wood meeting jawbone still rolling through the air, Boris ran into the shop and took a swing at Ross. He was still a bit slow on his feet after the fall from the train, however, and couldn't reach Ross before the blacksmith set his sights on him.

Ross and Boris ran at each other like a couple of rams that were about to lock horns. Rather than butt heads, however, the two men put their own weapons to use. Boris drew his gun and pulled his trigger, but not before Ross got to him and slammed his handle against Boris's ribs.

The pistol barked once, filling the shop with thunder and causing Eclipse to test the strength of the gate of his stall. Boris let out a pained groan that came all the way up from the bottom of his lungs.

Although Ross had no way of knowing the punishment Boris had taken recently, he could tell the man was hurting from a lot more than a single blow to the ribs. The blacksmith wasn't about to take the time to diagnose Boris's ills, so he sent another quick punch to the other man's ribs and turned back around to face Wilson.

By this time, Wilson was on his feet and getting ready to put Ross down the same way he'd sent Clint to the floor. Wilson had already gotten behind Ross, and would have introduced his club to the back of the blacksmith's head in another second. Ross's reflexes were just good enough for him to raise his arm and block Wilson's club with his handle.

Wood knocked against wood with a sound that wasn't nearly as loud as the gunshot from a few moments ago. That gunshot had punched a new hole in the floor, while Wilson's club was doing a whole lot more to turn the tide of the fight.

"Shoulda done what I told you to," Wilson snarled as he leaned into the blacksmith and put some muscle behind his club. "Now you're gonna have to pay just like this asshole here. Only difference is that I don't care if you wake up."

As he spoke, Wilson ground his club along the hammer's handle until he met up with Ross's fingers. From there, Wilson applied more pressure until he could see the other man wincing in pain.

At first, Ross thought he could grit his teeth through the

pain of his fingers being squashed under Wilson's club. But soon, it felt as if his bones were being ground beneath a pestle. He knew it wouldn't be long before one of those bones snapped under the pressure.

Ross let out a scream as he brought his knee up and pulled his arms to one side. He didn't know where he hit Wilson, but the impact caused the club to swing away from his fingers.

"Are you gonna help me?" Wilson growled as he took a step back and swung at Ross's head.

The end of his club connected with the blacksmith's face, but that was only enough to stoke the fire in Ross's belly. Blood trickled from his mouth as Ross gripped his makeshift weapon in both hands the way an executioner wielded an ax.

Tossing his club to his left hand, Wilson gripped his pistol with his right.

"No!" Boris hissed. "Put that gun away!"

Wilson took his eyes off Ross to face his brother with a look of pure disbelief etched into his face.

"Someone's coming," Boris said through gritted teeth.

Shaking his head, Wilson shifted his eyes back to the blacksmith so he could take his shot. He'd missed his opportunity, however, because Ross swung his handle to connect solidly with Wilson's gun hand.

The pistol went off on impact, but Wilson held onto it through sheer force of will. Before he could fire again, he was being dragged from the shop by his brother.

"Let go of me, God damn you!" Wilson snapped.

Boris tossed Wilson outside and shoved him toward the street. "Too much noise! That's why we didn't go in shooting in the first place!"

Now that he was outside the shop, Wilson could see the figures in the street. Some of them were simply craning their necks to get a look at what had happened, but a few were walking toward the blacksmith's shop.

"Everything all right over there?" one of the people asked.

Wilson put on a smile that looked more unnerving than anything else. "We're just fine. Honest mistake."

"Was that a gunshot?"

"My brother just knocked some things over," Wilson insisted. "No problem."

"Need any help?"

But the brothers were already hurrying down the street. By the time anyone got close enough to get a look inside the shop, the Nagles were rounding a corner.

TWENTY-SIX

Clint felt like he was falling through open air.

Soon, he felt like he was also rolling and spinning while still falling like a rock. Those elements combined to bring Clint's most recent meal up to his throat and then out of his mouth.

"There you go," Ross said. "Let it all out."

Clint coughed and spat the rest of the bitter fluid from his mouth. He peeled his eyes open enough to see he wasn't falling, but that didn't stop the sensation from working its way through his system. "What the . . . ?" he groaned.

"You took a knock on the back of the head," Ross explained.

"Where am I?"

"You're on my floor right now. I was about to get you to someplace a little more comfortable when you gave this spot a new coat of paint."

Wiping the rest of that "paint" from his mouth, Clint said, "Sorry about that."

"Think nothing of it. There's been worse. I keep horses in here, remember?"

That was enough to remind Clint of where he was. He

sat up, wavered slightly, and would have fallen over again if Ross hadn't been there to prop him up. "How long have I been here?"

"Not too long at all," Ross replied. "In fact, I was about to fetch the law."

"Don't."

"Pardon me?"

"Don't get the law," Clint insisted. "Unless they've already caught those two, it'll be too late to do anything about it."

"They might be caught once I get the law to help," Ross insisted.

"And then those brothers will probably pay their fine and get out. Once they're out, I'll be gone and they'll head over to . . . let's just say they'll pester a very nice woman to find out where I am. No," Clint said as he shook his head. The motion made him feel as if he'd just spun in a circle for a solid hour. "No law."

"All right then," Ross grumbled. "What would you do in your condition? Chase after them? I'd like to see you walk a straight line first."

Clint tried to get to his feet, but failed miserably. With a helping hand from the blacksmith, he was able to get his legs under him and then find his way to the milking stool Ross had used earlier. After placing his head in his hands, Clint pressed his palms to his eyes and forced the spinning to stop.

"You feeling steady enough for me to let go?" Ross asked.

It wasn't until that moment that Clint even realized the blacksmith had his hand on his shoulder. "Yeah," Clint said. "Let's give it a shot."

Ross took his hand away, but kept it close by in case it was needed. "You still all right?" he asked.

"Sure. Now I can feel every bit of the crack running through my skull."

"It ain't that bad," Ross said. "The bleeding's even stopped. You must have a hard head."

"Did you see me get knocked out?" Clint asked.

"Not quite. By the time I walked in here, you were down and one of them others was standing over you."

Keeping his head hanging low, Clint reached up with both hands to pat his pockets. He made the rounds from his shirt to his jeans and back again. When he placed his hands on his knees, Clint looked up with a pained grin. "Did you notice if that fellow took anything from me?"

Ross thought it over and then snapped his fingers. "Yeah! That fellow had his hand in your shirt pocket. Did he steal something?"

"Yep, but that's not exactly a bad thing." Clint started to get up, wobbled a bit, and then forced himself to his feet. "Can you do me a favor and get Eclipse ready to ride?"

Ross crossed his arms, chuckled, and looked at Clint in disbelief. "First of all, that stallion should be going easy for a while. Secondly, you should be going even easier. Maybe that fellow knocked your head a little harder than I thought."

Straightening his back, Clint pulled all of his concentration together so he could stand tall without wavering. "Eclipse needs to get moving, but he'll be loaded onto a train. We're headed south and once we're there, I'll be sure to go easy on him."

"All right," the blacksmith said. "What about you?"

"I'm going on the train, too. Whether I'm sitting there or here, it doesn't really matter. Besides," Clint added as he walked slowly to Eclipse's stall, "when did you become a doctor?"

Ross threw up his hands. "Just trying to look out for my fellow man is all. Forget I said a word."

Clint turned around and pulled in a breath to fight the dizziness that caused. "You may have saved my life," he said earnestly. "Believe me when I tell you I won't forget that. If there's anything I can do . . ."

"Just don't get yourself killed in my shop," Ross replied. "It'd be bad for business."

"Agreed."

"By the way, what did those assholes steal from you?"

"It wasn't much, but it should be enough to get those men out of Dallas for a while."

"Then maybe you should rest up. At the very least," Ross added, "your horse could do with some more time to heal."

Clint was at Eclipse's stall and rubbing the Darley Arabian's nose. Already, Eclipse seemed less willing to accept the attention and was more anxious to get out from within those walls. "I know you mean well," Clint said, "but Eclipse needs to get some wind in his face. For that matter, so do I."

"He'll be ready in an hour," Ross said grudgingly. "That quick enough for ya?"

"Should be just fine."

TWENTY-SEVEN

Clint still felt like he was spinning. He also felt like he was in the bottom of a sifter and being jostled along with the rest of the rocks and dirt as someone else looked for gold. The main difference between now and when Clint had first opened his eyes after being knocked out was that he really was being jostled. The spinning, on the other hand, was still in his head.

Olivia sat next to him on the train, tending to him by dabbing a cloth on the slick wound on his head. "That looks terrible, Clint," she said. "How does it feel?"

"It'd feel a lot better if you'd stop poking it," he snapped.

Pulling her hand back, Olivia dropped into her seat and looked at him quietly. That lasted for a few seconds before she extended her arm to dab at him some more. "Let me just clean you up a bit," she said.

Although Clint wanted to move her hand away, he knew that would only cause more discomfort than it prevented. "You've been cleaning me up since we got on board. I'm about as clean as I'm going to be."

She dropped back against her own seat and looked

around. Rather than the bench their last tickets had purchased, they now rode in a small compartment that they had all to themselves. The compartment didn't give them much more than a few seats and their own window, but the door separating them from the rest of the passengers went a long way for Clint's peace of mind.

"I don't think we should have gotten on this train," Olivia said. "If Wilson stole the ticket we bought earlier, that means they know where we're headed." Lowering her voice as if the walls around her were made of paper, she added, "They could be on this train."

"I know," Clint replied in a whisper that matched hers. "That's what I'm counting on."

"But after what happened . . ."

"What happened," Clint told her, "was a big mistake on Wilson's part. If they were going to bushwhack me like cowards, they should have killed me. Now, they've tipped their hand and I know what to expect from them. They won't be able to sneak up on me like that again."

"You can't be sure about that," Olivia said.

Clint reached back to touch the wound on his head. Although it looked gruesome and had bled enough to soak through to the collar of his shirt, it was more a source of headaches than anything else. "Yeah," he said intently. "I'm real sure about that."

"So what happens if the Nagles find out you're on this train?" she asked. "Do you think they'll give you the chance to throw them off again?"

"Considering they took a hell of a good run at me not too long ago, I'd say they'll keep their heads down and pray I don't find them."

"But . . ." Olivia said cautiously, "they got the drop on you and got away with it."

"And after all of that, I'm still up and about. What's more, I haven't even changed my itinerary. That lets them know their best isn't good enough. Believe me, it'll send a message."

Olivia looked over at the urn, which rested in its own spot on the seat across from her. The clay jar had dried up so the seal could barely be seen. It now looked like it had been made as one piece, and even the sounds of Abner McKay rattling around inside it could barely be heard.

"You don't think they'll stop coming at you, do you?" she asked.

"Nope."

"We've still got to ride the rest of the way on horseback. Even if they're not on this train, we'll all be starting from that train station. Whether the Nagles get there before or after we do, it won't take much for them to catch up to us. It's open country out there, Clint."

"I know. I've ridden it plenty of times myself."

"So you intend on letting them find you? If you keep giving them the first shot at you, one of these times they'll get lucky. I've played enough poker to know that everyone gets lucky some time or another."

Clint looked over at her and rubbed Olivia's cheek. There were no tears on her face, but he ran his finger over her skin just to savor the smooth texture of her. "I don't intend on getting either of us hurt. All that open country will work to our advantage because there won't be many places for them to hide. They already got lucky, but now I know what to expect. So long as they know where to go and we're there to lead them for a ways, it'll keep those two occupied so they won't be able to hurt us or anyone else."

"Do you think they're on this train?"

"Maybe," Clint said as he got up and went to the door. "But they won't be able to get us in here. Besides, all they got from me was that ticket. They're not stupid enough to make their move until they have something more to tell them where to go for whatever they're after."

"So we just wait?"

"Yeah," Clint said with a smirk.

"What are you doing?" Olivia asked.

The latch on the door to their compartment wasn't very strong. In fact, even after Clint had fitted the latch into place, the door still rattled within its frame as the train kept rumbling over the tracks.

"I'm locking us in," he replied.

Smiling carefully, Olivia adjusted her position in her seat so she had her back to the window and was facing Clint. "You want to keep us safe?"

Clint shrugged. "That, too."

"What other reason would you have?"

"I didn't want to get in trouble with Jenny, but now we're alone."

"And on the run," she reminded him. "You're still hurt."

"Of course I am and I'm healing up nicely. In the meantime, I believe I still need to collect on winning that race to those telegraph wires."

TWENTY-EIGHT

Boris Nagle sat on the end of a rickety bench bolted to the floor of the train's third passenger car. He kept his arms crossed and his hand within easy reach of his pistol. His eyes constantly darted from one spot to another, glancing nervously from the window to the other passengers to the doors at the front and back of the car.

When the door connecting the third to the second passenger car opened, Boris made a reflexive grab for his gun. He let out the breath he'd been holding when he saw who'd stepped into the car.

Although Wilson didn't look happy, he didn't go for his pistol when he spotted his brother. He slid along the bench facing Boris and glared at the preacher sitting there until the meek little man stood and moved to another spot.

"You seen either of them yet?" Boris asked.

"No, so you can take your hand away from your gun."

Boris nodded, but didn't move his hand. "Did you check out the rest of the train?"

"No."

"Then maybe I should."

"You should just sit here and keep your damn mouth

shut," Wilson snapped. "And take a few breaths. You look like you're about to piss yourself."

Chuckling unconvincingly, Boris took his hand away from his holster and rested it under the window. "Yeah," he said. "That gunman Olivia hired is the one that's probably about to piss himself right about now."

"I doubt it."

"Why?"

"Because he's not just some hired gun," Wilson replied.

"How do you know?" Glancing around at the passengers one more time, Boris leaned forward and whispered, "Did you hear something back in Dallas?"

"Yeah, when I was getting settled in at that blacksmith's shop. I heard him mention a name."

"What name?"

Wilson clenched his jaw and took a look around for himself. When he saw the same batch of uninterested faces pointing in other directions, he said, "Clint Adams."

Boris was dead quiet. He then furrowed his brow and asked, "Who?"

"You never heard of Clint Adams?" Wilson asked. Seeing the blank stare coming from his brother, Wilson added, "The Gunsmith?"

Finally, a spark of recognition showed upon Boris's face. "Aww, Jesus," he muttered.

"Yeah."

"You think he's on this train?" Boris asked.

"His horse is."

"Should I . . . ?"

"No," Wilson snapped. "Don't touch the horse. Just keep your eyes open."

Neither of the two said much after that. Boris stayed in his seat and Wilson sat across from him. Both kept watch on the doors and neither let his hand stray too far from his gun.

TWENTY-NINE

Olivia was standing with her body pressed against Clint. She ran her leg up along his and slipped her hands over his sides. Soon, she leaned forward so her cheek brushed against Clint's face as she slipped her hand between his legs.

"You like that?" she purred. Before Clint could answer, she'd started rubbing his growing erection. "Oh, I guess you do like that."

"Hold on," Clint said.

Looking at him with a shocked expression, she asked, "You sure you want me to stop?"

"I didn't say stop, I just said hold on." From there, Clint moved away from the door and picked up the small chair that had been resting next to the window. Since the cramped compartment was mostly filled by the other seats, that chair seemed to be a feeble attempt at decoration more than anything else. Still, it was sturdy and fitted nicely against the door and beneath the handle.

"There," Clint said. "Now, where were we?"

Olivia smiled and placed her hands flat on his chest. She guided him toward one of the main seats and then pushed him gently onto it. Turning around to the other seat, she picked up the clay jar and set it in a corner.

"Sorry, Uncle Abner," she said while [...] dress and then tossing it over the jar. "B[...] see this."

"That's a bit odd," Clint said as he looke[...] clothes.

Olivia was already on her knees and pul[...]g Clint's jeans down. "Really?" she asked while stroking his cock and then rubbing it against her lower lip. "You want me to stop?"

"Not hardly."

Smiling eagerly, she opened her mouth and slid her tongue all the way down Clint's rigid penis. She kept one hand wrapped around him and then wrapped her lips around his column of flesh so she could let every inch of it pass between her lips.

Once Clint was able to open his eyes, he saw that only one of Olivia's hands were still on him. Her other hand had slipped between her legs so she could rub herself in rhythm with the way she was sucking him. Clint slid his fingers through her hair and guided the rhythm of her bobbing head.

When she slowly lowered her mouth all the way down to the base of his cock, Clint was taken by surprise. He couldn't even make a sound as she held her mouth there and made slow motions with her tongue.

Olivia raised her head and looked him in the eye. "You won the bet," she whispered. "What do you want now?"

Clint stood up and put his hands on her hips. The only things Olivia wore were her stockings and a pair of lacy panties. He didn't say a word as he turned her around and stood behind her. Clint reached around to place his hands flat on her belly and then slide them along her smooth skin until he was cupping her breasts.

Arching her back, Olivia let out a slow sigh and reached over her shoulder and touched Clint's hair. Turning to look behind her, Olivia kissed him passionately as his hands moved slowly along her bare skin.

The more Clint kissed her, the harder he got. His erection pressed against Olivia's tight buttocks, and she wriggled her hips to excite him even more. Once Clint cupped her pert breasts in his hands, he teased her nipples between his thumbs and forefingers.

Keeping one hand on her breast, Clint reached between her legs with his other hand. Olivia's pussy was warm and wet. She sighed gratefully when he slipped a finger along her moist vagina, and sighed even louder when he slipped that finger inside.

Soon, Olivia wasn't just wriggling against him. She was writhing and pressing back against him as if using her body to beg him for more. She didn't have to plead for long before she felt Clint guide her to the window using one hand upon her shoulder.

Olivia placed her hands flat against the wall on either side of the window. The landscape rolled past the window, but she closed her eyes and waited for Clint to go further. When she felt his hands settle on her hips, Olivia spread her legs a bit wider. The next thing she felt was Clint's rigid cock easing into her from behind.

"Oh, Clint," she breathed. "Oh, my God."

Clint held onto her hips and let his eyes wander along the gentle slope of her back. Olivia's body was trim and smooth. Her shoulders were tense and her tight backside was raised slightly to accommodate him. As he slowly eased into her, Clint could feel Olivia's pussy tightening around him. By the time he'd pushed all the way inside, he could feel her entire body trembling with anticipation.

Unable to make her wait one more second, Clint gripped her hips and pulled her toward him as he thrust into her again. This time, he didn't linger in one spot. He pumped in and out of her in a rhythm that picked up pace as if he was purposely trying to steal her breath away.

Olivia's hair flowed along her back and tickled the base

of her spine. Whenever she felt Clint's grip tighten around her, she smiled and groaned appreciatively. Soon, she arched her back as much as she could and pushed against him so he could bury his cock in her as far as it would go. When he reached that limit, Olivia clenched her eyes shut and was overtaken by a powerful orgasm.

Clint smiled and stayed still as Olivia writhed with pleasure. Once her trembling stopped, she let out a breath and leaned forward as if the window was the only thing holding her up.

"I'm not through with you yet," he told her.

Olivia smiled and allowed herself to be turned around. Settling her backside against the windowsill and spreading her legs, she said, "Yes, sir."

Positioning himself between her thighs, Clint rubbed her glistening pussy until Olivia reached down to guide him into her. Clint moved his hips forward and felt his cock slide along her fingers before entering her once again.

Clint reached down to cup her backside in both hands. Pulling her close, he buried himself in her and then pumped a few times for good measure.

Olivia wrapped her arms around the back of Clint's neck and licked the side of his neck. Her entire body responded to every one of his moves. When she felt him lift her off the windowsill, Olivia wrapped her legs around him and locked her ankles against the small of his back.

Although Clint didn't carry her far, he was the only thing holding her off the ground. If that concerned Olivia in the slightest, she didn't show it. Instead, she ground her hips against him and moaned softly as he pumped in and out of her. He continued thrusting as he carried her to the middle of the room. Before he could set her down, he felt her entire body trembling with another impending climax.

Clint gripped onto her tightly and thrust into her a bit harder. Olivia leaned back and pumped her hips as well until she bit down on her lower lip and shuddered in his arms. The sight of her along with the feel of her clamped around him was enough to bring Clint to the edge as well. All it took was a few more deep thrusts and he was exploding inside her.

"Damn," she sighed. "I've got to lose more bets to you."

THIRTY

The train left them at a small town that looked as if it had been built around the station. Several buildings were clustered around the station, but there were fewer and fewer as the town stretched away along the tracks. Clint and Olivia stepped off the train cautiously. Their eyes darted back and forth in search of any sign of trouble.

Even though Clint was ready for just about anything, he felt the knot in his stomach tighten as more time went by without a single hitch.

"You think they're not on the train after all?" Olivia asked.

Clint shook his head. "That's too much to hope for."

"But that doesn't mean it's impossible."

"It's not impossible," Clint admitted. "But things seldom go that smoothly. There's plenty of ways to step off the train without being seen. They could have gotten off at the previous stop or they might be waiting for the next one. Neither one would add much to their ride since there's only a few miles between here and each of those stops."

Hefting her single bag, Olivia muttered, "I like my notion better."

Clint chuckled and walked toward the livery car. "So do I."

Even though he'd checked on Eclipse several times throughout the train ride, Clint held his breath until he saw the Darley Arabian being led down the ramp to the platform. Eclipse was hobbling a bit, but no more than could be expected considering what he'd already been through. Despite the fact that the stallion had been well cared for, Clint was anxious to get him away from the train.

"There's my girl," Olivia said when she saw Zel being led down the ramp.

"Are you going to tell me where we're headed?" Clint asked.

Olivia shook her head without taking her eyes from the tan mare. "Not yet. Too many eyes and ears around here."

Glancing about, Clint had to admit she was right. In fact, he was glad she'd been more cautious than he was.

"Let's buy some supplies and be on our way then," Clint said as he draped the saddlebags over his shoulder and led Eclipse toward the street.

"Should we wait and see if the Nagles show up?"

Clint shook his head. "If they're hidden, they won't show themselves here. If they already got off the train or will get off at the next stop, waiting around will only make it easier for them to catch up."

Olivia nodded at that, and became even more anxious than Clint to leave once they had their supplies bought and paid for. They were in that town for less than an hour when she was chomping at the bit to get out of there.

Knowing they needed to go south if they were to reach the Rio Grande, Clint looked out in that direction with his hand held up to shield his eyes from the sun. "Looks like flat country for at least a few miles," he said.

"Isn't that what I told you?" Olivia asked.

"Yeah, but I can't exactly do much planning before I get a look for myself."

"What are you planning? You don't even know exactly where we need to go."

"That's not what I'm thinking about," Clint said. "I'm more concerned with a good way to throw anyone off our track."

"You mean the Nagles?"

"Not just them," Clint replied. "Not unless there were three brothers instead of just the two."

Olivia thought about that for a moment, but still seemed confused. "No. There's always been just Boris and Wilson. What are you getting at?"

"There were two men who fired at us back in Labyrinth," Clint reminded her. "I killed one of them and it wasn't Boris or his brother. That means they've scrounged up some help before."

"You think they might do that again?"

"Now would be the time for it," Clint said. "It doesn't take a master strategist to know how difficult it could be to keep up with us once we get a head start. Since they haven't shown up yet, I'd say they're not too worried about catching up to us later."

Olivia folded her arms tightly across her chest and looked nervously up and down the short street. "You think someone else is keeping watch on us?"

"Either that, or one of those brothers is pretty confident in their tracking skills."

"Or," Olivia said hopefully, "they could have decided to give up and just forget this whole thing."

Clint looked at her with one raised eyebrow. He didn't have to watch her for long before Olivia shifted her eyes away from him.

"Just a suggestion," she said quietly.

"I admire your optimism," Clint said. "I just wish I could share it."

Shaking her head, she grudgingly replied, "I'm glad you don't. Otherwise, there wouldn't be any reason for you to come along on this excursion."

"Excursion, huh? Is that what we're calling it?"

Olivia brightened up and smiled warmly. "Yes," she said as she lifted her chin and straightened her back proudly. "Abner would have liked that."

"Then, excursion it is. After all, this ride is in his name."

"So should we get going or wait to see if we get ambushed?"

"Which way do we need to go?" Clint asked. "Or do you still want to keep it a secret?"

"Abner grew up in a place named Coldwater Rock. It's southwest of here."

"Good," Clint said. "Those hills due south of here aren't too far away and they should provide some cover if we spot anyone coming after us. Once we reach them, we should be able to use that terrain to cover our tracks as we turn to the west."

"Sounds good. Want to race?"

Clint scowled at her a bit as he looked down toward Eclipse's bandaged leg.

"Sorry," she said with a wince. "Maybe we can think of another bet along the way."

THIRTY-ONE

The town was called Elston. It was located a few miles farther along the railroad tracks from the spot where Clint and Olivia had gotten off. Those few miles seemed to drag by on leaden feet as Boris and Wilson sat glued to their window.

"You're sure it ain't far from here?" Boris asked the conductor for what must have been the twentieth time.

With his patient smile intact, the conductor nodded. "We'll be there any moment. There's plenty of small towns along the way here that sprouted up when the railroad purchased—"

"Spare us the damn history lesson," Wilson growled.

The conductor nodded and said, "It's a small place, so you might not see it coming from the window. In fact, we wouldn't have even stopped there if you hadn't paid to extend your tickets."

It wasn't long after that conversation that the train shuddered to a stop at the broken-down excuse for a station. All the other passengers looked around as if they were being robbed or the train had experienced some sort of problem.

Boris and Wilson got up and rushed to the door. When

they saw their horses being led from the livery car, the brothers nearly dragged the animals out by their manes. Once they were done with the train, Wilson headed for the nearest saloon.

"What are you doing?" Boris asked. "Now's not the time for a drink!"

"I ain't after any whiskey," Wilson replied. "How much money you got?"

"If you don't need whiskey, then what—"

"How much do you got?" Wilson roared.

His brother's tone caused Boris to reflexively shut his mouth and start patting his pockets. "Right around twenty dollars," he sputtered.

Wilson snatched the money from his hand and flipped through it. By this time, they'd arrived at the hitching post in front of the saloon. "Stay with the horses," Wilson said. "If you see that bitch or Adams, start shooting."

"They won't be headed this way," Boris said confidently. When he didn't get a reply from his brother, Boris started to fidget and asked, "Will they?"

Stomping into the saloon, Wilson found about what he'd been expecting: a few lonely drunks and some rough characters huddled around a card table. "I'm looking to hire a guide," he announced.

Nobody spoke up, but the barkeep made his way to the end of the bar that was closest to the door.

"You want anything to drink?" the barkeep asked.

Wilson dismissed him with an impatient wave of his hand. Taking a few more steps into the place, he held up a wad of money and asked, "Ain't there anyone in here who wants to earn this?"

That caught the attention of everyone else in the place. Eventually, one of the drunks pushed himself away from the bar and stepped forward.

"I know this area better than most," the drunk said. "Where you looking to go?"

"I'm tracking someone to the Rio Grande," Wilson said. "You know where along the Grande?"

By this time, the rough characters who'd been playing cards had made their way to the bar. There were three of them in all. Each of them looked to be in their late twenties. Each of them wore a gun, and not one of them looked as if they'd had any water splashed on their faces for at least a month.

"You men look like enterprising sorts," Wilson said. "Who wants to earn some money?"

The drunk stuck out his chest and stepped in between Wilson and the other men. "How much you offerin'?"

"All of it," Wilson said as he shook his fistful of cash.

"How much is it?"

"Fifty now and another hundred later."

The cardplayers looked back and forth among themselves before their self-appointed spokesman asked, "What do we have to do?"

Wilson cocked his head slightly. "There may be some rough spots along the way. You men opposed to dirty work?"

"No."

"Fine. Prove it. I want this old-timer to be bleeding at my feet within the next minute."

The dirty-faced men scowled at Wilson as the old drunk backed away.

"I don't have all day," Wilson said. "Are those guns around your waists just for show?"

The barkeep leaned over the bar and slapped a worn piece of lumber across Wilson's chest. "Now hold on here," he said. "I don't want any trouble in here. You should leave."

Before Wilson had a chance to say a word, the fellow who spoke for the dirty-faced men grabbed the long piece of wood from the barkeep and used it to shove him against the shelf of bottles behind the bar. Another one of the cardplayers stepped forward and punched the older drunk in the stomach. When the old man tried to fight back, the cardplayer drew his gun and slammed it against the back of the drunk's neck.

The spokesman for the cardplayers cracked the drunk across the face with the bartender's club. When he didn't see any blood right away, the spokesman savagely hit the drunk again. This time, the drunk hacked up blood as well as a few teeth.

Having knocked a few bottles from the shelf behind him, the barkeep bent to retrieve something else from under the bar. The weapon he chose was several steps above a piece of wood.

Wilson spotted the sawed-off shotgun in the bartender's hands and reacted immediately. He drew his pistol and fired a quick shot at the bartender. His bullet shattered a bottle on the shelf and punched a nice hole into the wall.

Trembling from the gunshot that had just exploded a few feet in front of him, the barkeep twitched nervously between the gun in Wilson's hand and the fresh hole in his wall.

"You got lucky with that first shot," Wilson growled. "Don't push it."

Cursing under his breath, the bartender lowered the shotgun until he could set it on the bar. From there, he raised his hands and tried not to look down the barrel of the gun being aimed at his face.

"You and you," Wilson said as he pointed to the spokesman and the cardplayer who'd drawn his pistol, "are hired." Shifting his sights to the cardplayer who hadn't laid a hand on the drunk, Wilson said, "You can stay here."

"We better get our money," the spokesman said.

Wilson grabbed the man's hand and slapped the money into it. "There's more to come."

"And if there's more blood to be spilled, we'll expect to be paid on top of that hundred."

"Don't you fellows worry about that," Wilson said as he headed for the door. "You men will have plenty of opportunities to earn a bonus like that."

THIRTY-TWO

"I don't like these men one bit," Boris groaned. He and his brother rode side by side and had put the town several miles behind them.

The two cardplayers Wilson had found in the saloon rode behind the brothers and had kept to themselves. Now, the more vocal of the two chuckled and said, "Then maybe you should pay us our money and we'll be off."

Wilson turned in his saddle and jabbed a finger at the two dirty-faced men. "You were hired to do a job and you're gonna do it. As for you," he said while turning toward his brother, "just keep your whining to yourself for a change."

"Amen to that," the second dirty-faced man replied.

"I liked you better when you kept your fucking mouth shut," Wilson said to that man. "You got something to say about my brother, you can keep it to yourself! Understand?"

The man went back to nodding quietly and didn't seem to be affected by Wilson's venomous tone.

"Hold up," Boris said as he raised his hand above his head. "I need to get a closer look at something. Wilson, why don't you come along with me?"

Wilson signaled for the other two to stay behind as he

followed his brother a few yards down the trail. When he got to where Boris was waiting, Wilson said, "Don't tell me you've started tracking."

Leaning forward and dropping his voice to an urgent whisper, Boris asked, "What the hell did you hire them for? They look like they'll rob us blind the first chance they get."

"They can't rob us because I already gave them our money."

"You did what?"

"It don't matter," Wilson said. "They've already earned it, and there should be more than enough to pay them the rest once we get what that old man left behind."

"And what if there ain't no money?"

"You know there's money. We both lived a stone's throw from that old fool since we were born and he's always had enough to get by. We both saw Abner getting more comfortable and we know he ain't the type to steal. His money wasn't in his house, so it's got to be somewhere."

"Maybe it's hidden somewhere else," Boris offered.

"We tore up every goddamn floorboard and tossed every last drawer in that house. There ain't nothing there. Hell, nobody even lives there no more, so that money's gotta be somewhere."

"And you're sure Olivia's got it?"

Wilson narrowed his eyes to glare at his brother. "If it wasn't Olivia McKay, you wouldn't even be asking that question. You're the one that was asked to mail them letters once Abner passed. Was there any letters mailed to anyone but Olivia?"

Reluctantly, Boris shook his head. "No."

"And were we told to keep an eye on anyone else but her?"

"No."

"That's right," Wilson said through gritted teeth. "We both helped that old fool through hard winters, we patched his roof, we got to watch him collect his money, and we didn't get a damn cent of it. Anyone else might've thought of us as kin, but that old man treated us like we was nothing! How many times did he set the law on our tails?"

After thinking it over for a few seconds, Boris shrugged and replied, "I don't know. Plenty of times."

"That's right! And that bitch Olivia gets to cheat at cards and Abner sends her more money to do it with. He owes us! He owes us, and we're taking that old bastard's money to make up for all the shit he threw our way all them years we lived in sight of that dirty fucking house of his!"

As his brother spoke, Boris set his jaw into a firm line and clenched his fists. "That's right."

"And what has Olivia ever done? She was a cock-tease when she came to visit Abner. She hit you when your back was turned. Now she cheats honest men at cards for a living. Why the hell should she get rewarded with some dead old man's money?"

"Yeah!"

Wilson nodded as if he was singing along to his own music. "And that son of a bitch she's riding with ain't no better," he said. "Just some killer who's made a name for himself because he can pull a trigger. So what? That don't mean he's entitled to any of that money either, because you know Olivia's using that to pay him."

"Probably."

Lowering his voice a bit, Wilson added, "If we need to hire some help, then so be it. I say that bitch is lucky we don't ride up to her like a stiff wind and cut her open until she tells us what we want to know. She's getting off light. Considering what her and her family's done to us, she's getting off real light."

Boris nodded and slapped his brother's shoulder. "You done good, Wilson. Sorry I doubted you."

"Forget about it," Wilson said merrily. "We can always shoot those two filthy drunks and take back our money anyways."

Although the smile was still on Boris's face and the fire was still in his belly, he couldn't help but feel a little queasy when he watched his brother pull back on his reins so he could rejoin the two men he'd hired. Despite the fact that he'd known Wilson his entire life, Boris couldn't tell if his brother was going to shake those drunks' hands or shoot them in the face.

"Did you mention something about a hired gun?" the first dirty-faced man asked.

"What was that?" Wilson replied.

"Up there with your brother. Did you say something about a gunfighter?"

Wilson shook his head and grinned. "Nobody you should worry about. He shouldn't be any problem for a man of your caliber."

When Boris looked at his brother, Wilson was snickering at the other two's expense.

THIRTY-THREE

The sun was low in the western sky and putting a comfortable warmth into the air. The ground was gritty but level beneath the horses' hooves, and a slow breeze rustled through the thorny branches on either side of the trail.

Olivia slipped her wide-brimmed hat off her head so it hung by the ribbon that looped under her chin. When she looked in Clint's direction, her eyes drifted down before coming back up to look at him.

"How's he doing?" she asked while nodding toward Eclipse.

Clint laughed and rubbed the stallion's neck. "He's ready to run. In fact, I feel like I'm sitting on a drawn bowstring."

"You want to stretch his legs?"

"Not if we don't have to," he replied. "Ross may have been a blacksmith, but he seemed to know more about horses than some professionals I've seen."

"He's a nice man," Olivia said with assurance. "Any man who's that good with animals has a good heart."

"That's awfully sweet talk coming from a professional cardsharp."

She chuckled and flipped a few stray strands of hair

from her eyes. "I don't let any of that sweetness get to the card table. Otherwise, I'd be broke."

Clint turned around in his saddle and surveyed the land around him. When he spotted a cluster of rocks not too far away, he steered Eclipse toward them and gave the reins a gentle flick. "Let's make camp over there," he said. "Those rocks should allow us to build a fire without the light carrying too far."

"I was thinking we should keep riding," Olivia said. "What if the Nagles are coming after us?"

"Even an experienced tracker would have gotten hung up for a while thanks to the precautions I've been taking. Besides, we should be able to hear anything bigger than a jackrabbit creeping up on us in this open country."

"I guess you're right. Still, I'd like to ride a little bit more."

"If you don't mind riding in the dark and risking a fall from your saddle from exhaustion," Clint told her, "be my guest. You'll also have to keep going alone. Eclipse has put enough wear on his bad leg."

When Olivia looked at the Darley Arabian, there was genuine pity in her eyes. "You're right. He looks worn out. Perhaps you should walk the rest of the way."

"Let's not get too eager with this pity nonsense," Clint said with a chuckle. "It may start to tarnish your talent as a gambler."

"I've only lost to you once," she reminded him.

"Sure, but the time I lost to you was after I'd already caught you red-handed."

She had to think that over for a second before nodding. "You've got a point there. Any reason why you insist on bringing that up?"

Clint chewed on that for a bit as Eclipse carried him closer to the rocks. Finally, he said, "Perhaps I'm just making sure you're not trying to put anything over on me now."

Olivia pulled back on her reins and waited for Clint to

notice. When he did, she remained rooted in place until Clint stopped and turned Eclipse around to face her.

"You don't trust me?" she asked.

"We've come a long way and blood's already been spilled, Olivia. Men have died and there's more lead to be set loose before this thing is done. If we're lucky, the both of us will ride away without too many scars to show for it. You may have played for high stakes and so have I, but in a game like that you can always tell when the end is drawing near. If I'm to see this thing through, I need to be certain of who I can count on."

"I may have been palming a card or two when we met," Olivia said. "I may have done some things in my life that I'm not proud of before we met. But have I ever given you reason to think you couldn't count on me?"

Clint looked her in the eye as she spoke and studied her carefully. Even the tone of her voice weighed heavily in his decision. Finally, he shook his head and said, "No, but it's good to hear you say that."

"What about you?" she asked as she studied him every bit as carefully. "Can I trust you to help me when there may be more trouble along the way?"

The fact that she'd asked that question so earnestly went even further in easing Clint's mind. "I came this far," he told her. "That means I've already decided on going the rest of the way."

THIRTY-FOUR

Clint and Olivia made camp a bit earlier than they would have preferred under normal circumstances. Eclipse seemed grateful to stop for the night, and was even more grateful once the saddle was taken from his back.

Olivia built a small fire, which was barely enough to heat a kettle and warm a skillet. While she put together as much of a meal as their situation would allow, Clint took a look at Eclipse's leg.

He wasn't a doctor, but Clint had spent enough time around horses to have learned plenty about them. Since Eclipse's ailment had already been diagnosed and resolved, all that remained was to make certain things kept progressing in the right direction.

"Take it easy, boy," Clint said as he gently unwrapped the bandages from Eclipse's leg. "Just taking a look."

The Darley Arabian seemed more interested in the grass sprouting from the ground than in what Clint was doing. As the bandages were removed, Eclipse shifted his weight and even lifted his leg so Clint could get a closer look for himself.

"How's it look?" Olivia asked from her spot near the fire.

Clint nodded and braced himself before placing a cautious finger over the wounded spot. When he didn't get kicked into next week, he said, "Seems like it's doing a lot better. It doesn't seem to hurt him as much."

"Good. That stallion is too pretty to be wounded. What sort of animal would do something like that to a helpless horse?"

"We know exactly what sort of animal did this," Clint replied.

"I know. Wilson used to cut up rabbits when he was a boy."

"You mean Boris?"

She shook her head. "Boris would catch them. He could trap them or even track them down to their holes, but Wilson was the one who would hurt them."

"So he's probably the one who did this to Eclipse," Clint said as he poured some clean water over some fresh bandages and wrung them out.

"No. If it had been Wilson, I doubt Eclipse would be standing there right now."

Clint stopped what he was doing as that notion drifted through his mind. Just the thought of someone hurting Eclipse had lit a fire in his belly. The idea of someone doing even more harm to the Darley Arabian struck a whole lot deeper. Shifting his thoughts from that dark spot, Clint wrapped the fresh bandages around Eclipse's leg and took a look at the hoof where most of the real damage had been done.

The leg had been bruised and cut a bit when Eclipse had been having trouble walking. Some of those scrapes had undoubtedly come from when the hobbler had been stuck into place, which made it difficult for Clint to think about something other than one of the Nagle brothers hurting his horse. It did Clint some good to see that the special shoe Ross had made was holding in place.

As if reading his thoughts, Olivia asked, "How's that foot looking?"

"Real good actually. This shoe is something to see."

Olivia stood up and walked over to him. Once she was next to Clint, she hunkered down and leaned forward as if she was trying to read small print in dim light. After what seemed to be a few solid moments of her studying the blacksmith's handiwork, she asked, "Is this the right shoe?"

"Yeah," Clint said with a laugh. "See how it's slanted a bit to take some of the weight off the spot that was wounded?"

"Uh-huh."

"And see here how these nails were spaced differently so they wouldn't bother the spot where Eclipse was hurt?"

"Uh-huh."

Looking over at her, Clint asked, "Do you really see any difference between this and another horseshoe?"

Reluctantly, Olivia shrugged and said, "No."

"Then why didn't you say so?"

"Because I didn't want to look foolish."

"Oh," Clint said as he lowered Eclipse's leg until the stallion adjusted his weight back onto it. "You're too late to avoid that."

Olivia waited until Clint was on his feet and a step away from Eclipse before she smacked his shoulder with the palm of her hand. The impact made some noise, but didn't do much more than put half a grimace on Clint's face.

"You're lucky that's all you got after that," she said.

"Really? And what else was I in store for if this wasn't such a lucky day?"

"You don't want to know."

Clint raised his eyebrows in a subtle challenge and replied, "Maybe I do."

"Don't push your luck, Clint Adams. I'm warning you."

"If you know as much about fighting as you do about horses, I think I like my chances."

Her eyes widened and her mouth hung open in exaggerated shock. Then, Olivia started to nod and circled him with her fists raised. "You want to test me? It's your funeral."

Clint laughed and started to walk away. He barely made it three steps before Olivia took a playful swat at his other shoulder. When he looked at her again, he saw the blatant challenge in her eyes.

"Oh, you're feeling tough now, huh?" Clint asked.

"I've felt tough ever since I beat you in that first card game."

"Really? Well, we'll see about that."

Clint circled her and made a few sharp half steps forward, but didn't move his hands from his defensive stance. Olivia, on the other hand, couldn't smile any wider as she took a few fast yet flailing swings at Clint's arms and shoulders.

"All right," she said as she cocked back her right fist. "Here it comes."

Clint let her cock her fist back as much as she wanted. He was waiting for her to make a real move. The moment she sent her arm forward, he stepped in and to the side. Clint was close enough to grab her arm and wrap his other arm around her waist before she could straighten her elbow.

She looked up at him with a smile. She was breathing a bit fast after their mock scuffle, but now her chest was heaving more from the excitement of finding herself in his arms. "That was a good move," she said.

Brushing his face against her smooth, black hair, Clint asked, "Were you really going to take a swing at me?"

"If you didn't grab hold of me soon, I was going to knock you out cold."

Clint cinched his arms around her and pulled her in tight against him. Olivia caught her breath and allowed her body to melt against him. When he moved his mouth closer to hers, she parted her lips in expectation of what he was about to do next.

The moment their lips met, a distant rumble drifted through the air. Both of them heard it, but neither one wanted to admit it.

"That sounds like horses coming this way," Clint said.

"Yes, it does."

They both knew they had to see if the Nagles had caught up to them. Even so, Clint kept his arms around her and kissed Olivia deeply while leaning her slightly back.

"Always leave them wanting more," he whispered after ending the kiss.

Olivia shook her head and kept her eyes closed. "I hate you."

THIRTY-FIVE

While Clint rushed to his saddlebags, Olivia kicked dirt onto the fire. She also managed to kick dirt into the frying pan, which still held some of the bacon she'd been cooking. Swearing under her breath, she moved the frying pan away while putting out the last of the fire.

Clint chuckled at the sight of Olivia's mad scramble, but he couldn't watch her for long. Instead, he took his spyglass from the saddlebag and made his way to the rocks that were between the camp and the sound of hooves thumping against the earth.

"Is it them?" Olivia whispered as she kept piling dirt onto the fire.

Stretched out on his belly with his legs hanging over the side of the rocks, Clint shifted so he wasn't getting jabbed too badly by a jagged piece of stone. "I can't tell yet," he replied as he raised the spyglass to his eye.

"What about now?" Olivia asked a few seconds later.

It took a few seconds for Clint to get his bearings and aim his spyglass at the right spot. The moment he caught sight of the horses in the distance, he held his breath so he could get the steadiest look possible.

"Clint? Is it them?"

He didn't say anything, simply because the slightest movement would have caused the spyglass to tremble enough to blur his view. With the light already fading by the second, Clint couldn't afford to make things worse by his own hand.

"Clint?"

"Give me a second," he hissed. "Just make sure there's no smoke coming from that fire."

Olivia looked down at the ground, and had to squint to distinguish any wisps of smoke from the shadows that were naturally there. Finally, her eyes adjusted well enough for her to tell him, "It's not too bad."

"Will anyone be able to see it from a distance?"

"No."

Just to be sure, Clint took a quick look over his shoulder. "Good," he told her before placing his eye once more against the spyglass.

Before long, Clint could hear scraping against the rocks. A second or two later, Olivia was settling in beside him.

"Keep your head down," he said while reaching out to place his free hand between her shoulders. "There isn't much light in the sky, but there could be enough for whoever's out there to see us before we can see them."

Olivia flattened herself against the rock and glanced nervously over her shoulder. The sky was mostly dark, but there was still a faint purple glow to mark where the sun had been before dipping below the horizon. She winced at the way the trees stood out against that soft glow, and could only hope she and Clint didn't stand out so well to the approaching riders.

"Do you think they spotted us?" Olivia whispered as she wriggled in close to him.

Clint took a moment before answering. He kept both arms propped against the rock so he could keep the spyglass as steady as possible. Every so often, he had to look away before all the different shades of black started to blend together. Finally, he said, "I don't know, but I do know they're headed this way."

The horses weren't moving at a full gallop, but that didn't make Clint feel any better. Although they wouldn't get to Clint and Olivia as fast, the whole group seemed to be moving carefully and methodically in the same direction as Clint and Olivia had been going. If they didn't know about the camp already, the riders seemed to be searching awfully hard for it.

"They seem so far away for us to be able to hear them."

"That's because there's four of them."

"What?"

Clint nodded and scooted a bit closer to the edge of the rock. "I don't normally have trouble counting that high, but I did it twice just to be certain."

"This isn't funny, Clint."

"I know, but I still can't tell if those horses are being ridden by the Nagle brothers or if they're just some other folks passing through."

"They might not be the Nagles?" Olivia asked hopefully.

"Maybe not," Clint replied. Before she could get her hopes up too high, he added, "Still, you'd better bring me my rifle."

THIRTY-SIX

As the horses drew closer, the sound of their hooves grew. Soon, the horses were close enough to the camp for Clint to hear the animals' breathing and the scrape of their shoes against the rocky ground a stone's throw from where the campfire had been.

"Damn," Boris snarled in a voice that was just as distinctive to Clint as the man's face. "How big of a lead did they get?"

The voice that responded was dry as the desert floor and prickly as an old cactus. "Couldn't have been too big of a lead if Adams is still trying to ride that horse of his."

"Who's Adams?"

Clint didn't recognize that voice, but it sounded more like a belch from a frog.

"Just one of the assholes we're after," the second voice replied. "That's all you need to know."

Clint still couldn't see the riders, but he could hear them coming around the rocks that he was using for cover. Actually, Clint was using an old blanket for cover. The tattered wool blanket had seen him through plenty of cold nights, but now it could mean the difference between watching the riders and trading shots with them.

Lying on top of the rocks as flat as he could, Clint remained still and hoped the old blanket was covering his boots. The blanket was draped over his face with about an inch to spare. Clint could only hope his feet weren't poking out the other side.

In the daylight, he might have been a comical sight. But with the purple hue fading across the sky and the shadows at their thickest, he was just another ripple along the top of the rocks. In fact, since he'd wedged himself in between two of the largest rocks, Clint might have seemed like the mortar that made the outcropping look like one huge boulder.

Olivia and the horses, on the other hand, were in a different sort of predicament. Although they were crouched down and hiding among a few nearby trees, they were less than fifteen yards from the original campsite. They had a blanket or two draped over them, but they had to rely mostly on natural cover.

If the riders didn't head for those trees or study them too carefully, they might never know anyone was there. If they let their eyes wander in that direction for too long, however, they wouldn't have much trouble picking their targets.

"Did they come through here?" the man with the rasping voice asked.

Boris was quick to reply. "How the hell can I know that, Wilson? I can barely see anything anymore."

"There's enough light to keep riding."

"But not enough to keep tracking. We should just make camp and head out at first light. For all we know, we might just lose their trail completely."

Clint already had his pistol in hand. His fingers tightened around the grip and he eased it toward the edge of the rocks. Although he moved his hands as slowly as possible, the sound of iron scraping against stone was a piercing shriek to his ears. By now, the sound of his own breathing seemed to echo beneath the blanket.

"They gotta be nearby," Wilson insisted. "They still got one lame horse among them, right?"

"It ain't lame, but it's hurt," Boris said.

"And you know that's one of the horses they're using?"

"I saw it in the livery car. I already told you that. I also saw some peculiar tracks that could have been left by a new shoe. I already told you that, too."

"I recall him saying that," the belching frog said.

Just then, one of the horses rounded the rocks and came into Clint's line of sight. Although he couldn't see all the details of the man's face, Clint could make out enough angles to know it wasn't the face of the man he'd fought on the train to Dallas.

"I gotta listen to my brother's smart mouth," Wilson snapped as he drew his gun and aimed it in one swift motion, "but I sure as hell don't gotta listen to yours."

Clint's eyes narrowed as he watched Wilson take aim. The motion had been quick and smooth. The look in Wilson's eyes left no room for doubt that he would pull his trigger if he was so inclined. The twitch at the corner of Wilson's mouth made it seem as if he was listening to the counsel of some voices only he could hear.

With every second that ticked by, Clint became more convinced that he would have to abandon his spot and take his chances with all four of them before they caught sight of Olivia. Fortunately, Wilson was demanding all of the attention for the moment.

"Fine," Boris said. "Let's keep moving."

"Can you see where we need to go or not?" Wilson asked.

"We know they're headed to the Rio Grande and they've been traveling southwest to get there. We can keep going in that direction and look for a camp. We could even spread out and cover more ground. If there's a fire lit, one of us'll be able to see it."

Since Clint wasn't about to move more than it took to breathe, he kept his eyes on Wilson. His next breath caught in the back of his throat when Wilson snapped his head around to look at Clint as if he could feel the heat from his stare.

As Clint lay wedged between the rocks, he became certain that he'd made a big mistake.

His gun was in hand and he could take a shot whenever he pleased, but that might not be enough to save Olivia.

Even after he'd killed Wilson, Clint couldn't see the others well enough to know for certain if he'd live to see the next couple of seconds after Wilson hit the ground.

And there was always the chance that Clint might miss with his first shot and then be killed by the hailstorm of lead that was sure to follow.

Being killed while stuffed between some rocks wasn't exactly the best sort of death he could have imagined.

All of that rolled through Clint's mind in the space of a few seconds. Those thoughts weren't silenced until Wilson finally blinked.

"We'll ride a little ways more," Wilson said as he shifted his glare to one of the other three men. "If we don't spot a fire soon, we'll make camp and get some rest. Will you be able to pick up their tracks come morning?"

"Yeah," Boris said. "Now, will you put that gun away?"

Wilson loosened his grip on the pistol so it dangled from his trigger finger. He then dropped the gun into its holster and pointed his horse toward the southwest. As soon as he flicked his reins, he was followed by the rest of the horsemen.

"Spread out from here," Boris ordered. "They can't be too much farther ahead of us. I don't even think their horses were moving that fast."

The four men rode away from the camp without more

than a passing glance tossed toward the trees. Clint didn't allow himself to exhale until the Nagles and their two partners were far enough away that the sounds of their horses could no longer be heard.

Clint couldn't get out from between the rocks fast enough. As soon as he stepped out, he saw Olivia raise her head and wave. Since he knew she and the horses were there, Clint wondered how the hell the others could have missed them.

"Well," Olivia said breathlessly as she walked over to Clint. "That was easy.

"Speak for yourself."

THIRTY-SEVEN

The sun's rays hadn't even put a dent into the inky blackness of the sky when Clint woke Olivia and started saddling Eclipse. He checked the Darley Arabian's bandages and found only a few specks of blood. After just a few minutes, the stallion seemed ready to run.

"Looks like that shoe's doing the trick," Clint said.

Olivia yawned and dragged her feet while loading up her bedroll. "Good. Maybe we can get some more sleep."

"No time for that."

"I thought we agreed this camp was still safe since the Nagles already passed through here."

"I told you it should be safe," Clint reminded her. "Not that I was certain about it."

"So you just let us sleep here anyway?"

Clint let out a deep breath and rubbed his eyes. "You slept. I kept one eye open to see if those childhood friends of yours would double back."

Walking back over to him, Olivia took Clint's hat from his head and tussled his hair. "Aww. That was sweet."

"You call it sweet. I call it not wanting to get shot in my sleep."

"Did you get any rest at all?"

"Yeah," Clint lied. "A little."

Judging by the way Olivia stared him down, she didn't believe him. Still, she wasn't about to call him on it just yet. "There's some coffee left over from last night. Why don't I make a little fire and heat it up for you?"

Clint shook his head. "The whole reason for getting up before sunrise was so we could get moving before those brothers do."

"The way they were fighting last night, they'll be at each other's throats until afternoon since they haven't found us yet. That should buy us more than enough time to have a nice breakfast."

After a bit of a pause, Clint asked, "Why don't we split the difference?"

"Which means I'll put a fire under this kettle. If you want, you can stretch out and rest your eyes while I get this ready."

"I need to keep watch."

"You need to get a bit of rest," Olivia insisted. "You won't do anyone any good if you fall out of your saddle or doze off when we do get closer to those Nagles."

"But if—"

"If someone comes around, I'll see them," Olivia told him. "I think I can manage pouring coffee and watching for horses at the same time."

Clint might have protested some more if he'd had enough wind in his sails. As it was, he leaned back against a rock and found it to be just as comfortable as a stack of mattresses. When he opened his eyes again, it was due to the smell of coffee directly under his nose.

Sitting bolt upright, Clint let out a rough breath and found himself looking directly at Olivia's smiling face. "If you offer to let me rest for a moment, the least you could do is let me rest," he said.

She nodded patiently and replied, "You've been out for almost an hour."

"What?"

Despite the fact that he felt as if he'd just stretched his legs out, Clint saw enough light in the sky to verify Olivia's claim. It would still be a while before the sun was completely up, but the rich red and orange hues didn't do much to improve Clint's mood.

"Damn," he grumbled. "I wanted to be on the trail by now."

"This is wide-open terrain," Olivia said. "I would have spotted anyone if they were within a mile of us. The only movement that's caught my eye has come from a snake or two."

Once he was on his feet, Clint took the coffee and drank it. Olivia had been true to her word, since the coffee barely felt warm. Even so, it was strong enough to get his eyes open a bit wider. Tossing the rest of the coffee out, Clint handed her the mug and said, "Let's get going."

"Next time, I should just let you fall from your saddle."

"Hopefully, there won't be a next time before we get to where we're going. How much farther is it anyway?"

"Even with Eclipse's bad leg, we could make it there by nightfall. Still, we might cross paths with Boris and Wilson."

"What's the name of the place again?"

"Coldwater Rock," Olivia replied. "I haven't been there for a while, though, so it might have changed names."

"Or it might not even be there. Small towns along a river tend to get washed away sometimes."

"If that's the case, then we've come a long way for nothing."

Clint studied her as he asked, "What's that mean? The main purpose of coming here is to scatter the ashes, right?"

Olivia nodded, but wasn't quick about it. "I've just been thinking. You know . . . about what we were talking about before."

"You mean about your uncle coming into some money?"

"Yes! I think the word must have gotten out."

"There's no other reason why these men would go through so much trouble to come after us. Perhaps they know something that we don't. Or," Clint added, "at least something that I don't."

Meeting Clint's gaze, Olivia told him, "I don't know how much, but Abner had to have collected some money. He was always into some venture or other. He gambled much better than I ever could and he was smart about his money. My guess would be for it to be somewhere in his house. Or maybe he sent it to Jenny. Maybe he left a will. I don't know, Clint."

"Those brothers must think we know something. Otherwise, they wouldn't need to track us."

"They'd shoot their own mother in the back just to get the rings off her fingers."

"I haven't known the Nagles for long," Clint admitted, "but I've seen enough to believe that much."

"And what about the rest? Do you still believe me about the money?"

The fact of the matter was that Olivia was smart enough to have figured out plenty of ways to get to that money on her own if she knew so much about it. One thing that spoke volumes to Clint was the way Olivia handled the clay jar containing her uncle's ashes.

So far, Olivia hadn't let that urn out of her sight. She'd insisted on carrying it herself and when she handled it, she did so as if she was cradling a newborn.

"I've been stabbed in the back plenty of times," Clint said. "Mostly, it was so someone could get their hands on money."

"I don't know what to tell you, Clint," she replied with a shrug. "If you don't trust me now, there's nothing more I can do."

"It's not a matter of trust. All I ask is that you tell me everything I might need to know."

"Abner might have stashed money somewhere or maybe the Nagle brothers just think he did. Boris might still be mad at what I did to him with that shovel. Wilson's just plain crazy. That's what I know."

"Where's Coldwater Rock again?"

"Southwest of here."

After a bit of hesitation, Clint nodded. "All right then. Like I said, we'll ride south from here and then cut west. Hopefully, that'll be enough to steer clear of the Nagles and their hired guns."

When Clint walked over to Eclipse, he heard Olivia keeping pace directly behind him. She tapped him on the shoulder and waited for him to turn around before speaking.

"You're not the only one that's ever been betrayed, you know," she said. "I've been lied to, cheated, and threatened with everything from being robbed to being killed. Some men would see a woman dead if they didn't get a friendly enough smile or if she dared to keep her legs crossed when he wanted them open. That," she said while pulling her skirts aside to reveal the derringer strapped to her right knee, "is why I keep this where I can always get to it. Always."

Clint knew about the derringer. He'd even known when she'd shifted it to another spot when she knew her leg wasn't exactly going to be covered. He also knew she didn't need to show him that gun. "It's good to see there's no secrets," he told her.

"And I'm glad you're such a cautious man," she replied. "That's why I'm so grateful you're with me now."

So far, Clint hadn't had much of a reason to think Olivia

was lying to him. He was glad that he still felt that way now. Even so, he knew better than to strike any possibility from his mind when lives were being threatened. Still, Olivia might have been a card cheat, but she struck him as trustworthy.

Of course, a man couldn't be too careful.

THIRTY-EIGHT

They rode south for a good portion of the day. For the first
few hours, it was a struggle for Clint to keep his eyes open.
Olivia's coffee had helped in that regard, but feeling the
crisp morning air in his face as he put Eclipse through his
paces truly woke him up.

It seemed the Darley Arabian was feeling better as well.
Not only was he quicker to build up speed, but his legs
pounded against the ground with less trepidation than before. Whether it was the shoe Ross had made or the time
the stallion had been given to heal, Eclipse was chomping
at the bit again.

Clint knew better than to give in to the horse's instinct
to gallop when he saw so much open trail in front of him.
Even Clint could feel that instinct when he thought about
beating the Nagles to their destination. Fortunately, Clint
and Olivia had a major factor still in their favor: The Nagles didn't know what their destination was. If they did,
they wouldn't have taken so long to get there. Despite that
fact, Clint wasn't about to rush when that might cause him
to run straight into the Nagles' sights.

The land beneath them began to shift from flat, rocky
terrain to rolling, sandy hills that looked like an enormous

quilt frozen in mid-ruffle. One of the higher swells was directly ahead and when they reached it, Clint and Olivia pulled back on their reins.

"There's the Rio Grande," Clint said.

Olivia looked to the west and shielded her eyes from the sun. "Coldwater Rock shouldn't be much farther. I'd say a few miles or so."

"You don't sound very certain."

"I've only been there a few times. And that was back when I was a little girl. I remember more about the water on my feet and the shapes of the clouds than I do about where I actually was."

"What *do* you remember?"

Olivia smiled fondly and looked up as if she was seeing those same shapes in the sky that had been there when she still had her hair in pigtails. "One summer, we were supposed to visit Abner. You see, he liked coming down here because he only had a few sisters left and they both lived in Coldwater Rock. Well, we couldn't go for some reason or another and I was upset. I wouldn't stop crying until my father showed me on a map how far away this was from home. Whenever Abner would go away, I would look at that spot on the map."

"That's a sweet story," Clint said, "Let's hope your father wasn't just pointing to some random spot along the Rio Grande to shut you up."

The smile remained on Olivia's face the way mud remained after being thrown against a wall. "Nice, Clint. Really nice. Next time I'll just keep my memories to myself."

Clint chuckled and pointed to the west. "So we just need to ride that way until we reach this town of yours."

"That's right."

"And what happens if there's nothing there?"

"What's that supposed to mean?" she asked with genuine anger written across her face.

"No offense meant, Olivia," Clint was quick to say. "It's

just that a kid's memory isn't exactly the most reliable thing."

"It's more than just a memory. I kept that map, and Abner showed me the same spot a few times. The last time I was here, he even showed me a bend in the river that marked where his house was."

"Really? That's a pretty important landmark. How long were you going to keep that under your hat?"

Olivia blinked and shook her head as if she was about to sneeze. "Actually," she said, "I just remembered that right now." She furrowed her brow and stared straight ahead. The concentration in her eyes made it clear that she wasn't exactly focused on anything Clint could see. "It was a kink in the river," she finally told him.

"A kink?"

Olivia nodded. "That's how I saw it. Abner called it a boot heel."

"What's it look like?" Clint asked.

After thinking for another few seconds, Olivia lifted one finger and traced a line in the air. "Like that. At least, that's what it looked like on the map."

"So it took a sharp turn toward the north, ran a little ways, and dipped back south again?"

"Yes," Olivia said proudly. "Yes, that's it. Does that help?"

"It sure does."

"Do you think we'll be able to see it?"

"Yeah," Clint said as he pointed toward the river in the distance. "We just might."

THIRTY-NINE

The Rio Grande sparkled with reflected sunlight, making the entire watery stretch look more like rough glass than a river. Although no river was too straight for too long, Clint and Olivia didn't have any trouble whatsoever in spotting the distinctive pattern of the Rio Grande as it turned and ran toward them a little ways, and then veered back around and down to turn once again along its previous course.

From their vantage on higher ground, the shape of the pattern looked like a large boot heel. On a map, the line might have looked more like a kink in a blue thread.

Seeing the boot heel and getting to it were two very different things. Once they were off the top of the hills, Clint and Olivia nearly lost sight of the distinctive shape. Since there was no town to catch their attention, both of them thought they'd latched onto the wrong boot heel.

Once they'd covered the next few miles, Olivia regained some of her confidence.

"There," she said while leaning forward and pointing at the river. "I see it."

Clint squinted and shook his head. "I don't see anything."

"It's all looking familiar now. Trust me. I can see the place. There's not a lot left, but I can see it."

Shrugging, Clint said, "All right. Lead the way."

Olivia was more than happy to do just that. She snapped the reins and almost left Eclipse in her dust. Fortunately, the Darley Arabian had worked himself up to something close to full speed throughout the course of the day and Clint was willing to stretch his legs a bit more.

Since they were headed in the right direction anyway, Clint was willing to follow Olivia whether he saw anything or not. In fact, since she took the lead, it freed him up to let his eyes wander along the horizon for any trace of the Nagles and their newly acquired partners.

As far as Clint could tell, he and Olivia were alone. Then again, he didn't allow himself to get too comfortable either. There were plenty of twists in the trail and several places where a small group of men could hide. It was no mistake that outlaws preferred going south when they wanted to escape from the law. Still, Clint wasn't going to give in to the tricky terrain by letting his guard down.

"You see it, Clint?" Olivia shouted from her saddle.

The question was almost lost amid the thunder of the two horses' hooves, but her enthusiasm pushed her words through the air well enough.

Clint hadn't spotted much of anything so far, and he was about to tell her that when he looked ahead. Before he could give the response that was on the tip of his tongue, he squinted and leaned forward. "I think I do see something," he said. "Looks like an old mining camp or something."

"It's Coldwater Rock," she shouted back to him. "I know it!"

When he saw her snap her reins, Clint shouted, "Slow down!"

"Come on, Clint! That's the place! I'll race you there."

Cursing under his breath, Clint snapped his own reins and felt an immediate burst of speed from Eclipse. He came alongside Olivia's tan mare, and stayed there just long enough for him to reach out and wave before grabbing the reins from her hand.

"I said slow down!" he ordered.

She pulled back on her reins, but didn't look happy about it. When she'd slowed to a trot, Olivia asked, "What's wrong with you? I thought you trusted me to get you here."

"I do," Clint replied. "And that might be the place. We also might still have four gunmen tracking us."

"Have you seen them?"

"No, but that doesn't mean they're not around. Just take a moment and think before you go charging in like a damn fool!"

Olivia looked ahead and then back at Clint. Then, she pulled back on her reins even more. "You're right, Clint. Sorry about that. I guess I just got a little excited."

"It's fine. Now, are you certain that's the place? It doesn't look like more than a few old buildings."

"It never was much more than that. Whenever I used to visit Abner here, I remember we had to go to a trading post for food and supplies. That was one of the first times I ever saw a real Indian."

Looking at the way Olivia's face brightened when she spoke, Clint couldn't help but smile. "You really have a lot of fond memories about your uncle, don't you?"

"Yes. I never saw him too much, but it was always good when I did. That's why I figure the least I can do for him now is see to it that he winds up where he wants to be."

"That's fair enough." Shifting his eyes to the trail ahead, Clint added, "It's not much farther before we get to that settlement. There's also not many ways for someone to ride in on us once we're there."

"What about that rise over there?" Olivia asked.

Clint looked toward the steep hill that she'd spotted. It wasn't very imposing, but the rise was capped by several clusters of jagged rocks that sat upon the crest like a crown.

"Yeah," he said. "That's the one spot that has me worried. If there's an ambush to be made, it'll be from there."

"Should we wait to see if the Nagles jump us first?"

"No. If they do decide to make a run at us, we'll see them coming. Things are a lot easier if you're prepared for the worst. Just don't make it any easier for the worst to happen."

"All right," Olivia said anxiously. "How long should we wait?"

"Let's go there now, but not so fast. There's the chance that they might already be there."

"I doubt that. I barely even knew where to find this place until I remembered that kink in the river."

"Don't remind me," Clint said grudgingly. "Riding alongside someone who'd come this far out on a hunch doesn't set well."

"You're not much of a gambler, are you?" she asked.

"You're only one out of two in our bets," he reminded her.

"Care to make it best two out of three?"

FORTY

Coldwater Rock couldn't have been a more appropriate name for the place Clint and Olivia found themselves in. The settlement was along the river where there were most definitely rocks. Scooping a hand into the Rio Grande, Clint was pleased to find the water to be refreshingly cool. Eclipse was actually more grateful for that.

Other than those few things, there wasn't much.

Clint stood with his hands on his hips and watched Olivia walk around the three buildings situated near the bank of the Rio Grande. "You're certain this is the place?" he asked. "There's nothing marking this as anything more than a camp."

"This is it," she replied with certainty. Olivia closed her eyes and took a few more steps without so much as stumbling over one of the rocks strewn along the ground. "I can almost smell the smoke from Abner's fire."

"Looks like there was plenty of smoke around here," Clint said as he ran his fingers along the charred side of the nearest building. "And plenty of fire as well."

Olivia opened her eyes and looked around again. This time, she saw more of what was there instead of what she'd remembered. "There was a fire. Looks like this whole place might have burned down."

"It was a long time ago," Clint said. "Most of this wood looks like it rotted after it was burned." Stepping inside the broken frame of the building, Clint took a quick look around. "This place is empty. That means it was probably abandoned even before it was burned."

"What a shame. This was such a quiet, happy place."

"For you maybe. I can't tell much from what's left, but this looks like a spot that was set up to do a job. There wasn't any store and I don't see anything that looks like a mill or even a waterwheel. That over there," he said while nodding toward a narrow, crumbling frame, "looks like it might have been a stable. It's barely big enough for four horses."

The longer Olivia looked around, the less she resembled the little girl she'd been the last time she'd walked along that path. Soon, it was obvious that she was seeing the same empty, broken buildings that Clint saw. "Abner's house was this one," she said as she raised a tired finger to point at the farthest structure.

Clint studied the terrain surrounding the abandoned settlement. The land was still just as quiet as the buildings. Satisfied with the calmness in the air, Clint rested his hand on his Colt and walked forward. The moment he saw Olivia start to move, Clint said, "Stay put. Let me take a look around first."

Although she was anxious to get into the remains of the house, Olivia stood her ground and let Clint go in.

There wasn't much for him to see. Like the other buildings, the roof had already been burned away, collapsed, or been swept up by the elements. More than likely, it was a combination of all three. The floor was relatively sturdy, but creaked as if it was in pain every time Clint set a boot down on it.

There had been at least two rooms in the place. The walls were mostly rubble, but there could have been another one sectioning off a third room. Either way, there couldn't have been much room inside that house. All he found inside were some things that had been washed up when the river had swelled, and a small animal's carcass in one corner.

"Come on in, Olivia," Clint shouted.

She was inside in a matter of seconds. Despite the condition of the place, she looked around with a fond smile on her face and a few tears in her eyes. "This is it all right. I only wish it was how I remembered it."

"Nothing hardly ever stays the way we remember," Clint said. "That's the nice thing about memories."

"It doesn't feel nice right now."

Just then, Clint realized that Olivia had taken the clay jar from her saddlebag. She held it in the crook of her arm as she wandered through the remains of the house. It didn't take her long to see it all.

"This is where I used to sleep," she said fondly as she stopped in one corner. "Even when I was a girl, I knew this was a pantry. Still, Abner used to fill it up with blankets and pillows so I could sleep in there. He said it was my own little bird's nest."

Clint felt more and more uncomfortable the longer they remained in the house. It was the sort of feeling someone would get if they stepped in front of a loaded cannon and stayed there to enjoy the scenery. That unsettled feeling in his gut paid off when he caught sight of two horses breaking from the crowned ridge he'd spotted earlier.

"I hate to cut this short, but I think those brothers have found this place as well," Clint said.

Olivia was kneeling in the space that had been Abner's pantry and was pressing her hand to the floor.

"Yep," Clint said as he looked out the window. "The other two are circling around on the east side."

"I'm not letting them chase us away from here," Olivia said. "Not after we've come this far."

"I agree. We should have enough time to scatter the

ashes before their horses meet up here, but we can't dawdle for very long." When he turned around to check on her, Clint found Olivia digging her fingers between the floorboards. "What are you doing? There's no time for this."

"There was something else in my letter," she explained. "It was just some little thing that I thought was in there to make sure I knew the message was from Abner."

"Olivia . . . they're riding awfully fast."

"It said for me to be sure and check the nest for eggs."

"We really don't have time for—"

Clint stopped when he heard the crack of splintering wood. He saw Olivia pull one of the boards up from the floor and hold it out to him triumphantly.

"It's still here!" she said. Turning her attention to the floor, Olivia reached into the hole to retrieve a few tarnished, broken combs and some dirty marbles. "This is where I stashed some of my things when I came to visit. I thought it was a big secret." When she reached into the hole again, she pulled out a flat bundle wrapped in leather and held together by several lengths of twine.

"What's that?" Clint asked.

Olivia stared at the bundle with wide eyes. "I don't know. I didn't put it here."

FORTY-ONE

Clint brought the horses into the old house so they could at least get some protection behind what was left of the walls. Once the horses were in place, Clint walked over to Eclipse, patted the stallion's neck, and took the rifle hanging from the saddle's boot.

"You figure out what you found yet?" he asked as he checked the rifle to make sure it was in proper firing condition.

"Yes. It's another letter from Abner."

"He sure did enjoy his correspondence," Clint said. He went to the window, and was quickly able to spot the four horses. They were converging on Coldwater Rock from two different directions, and had already covered half the distance between the crowned ridge and the house.

Walking around to the back of the house, Clint asked, "What's this letter say?"

"It says he knows that if anyone's reading this letter, it's me," Olivia replied in a trembling voice.

There weren't any more riders coming in from the back of the house, but that didn't make Clint feel too much better. They were, after all, still outnumbered two to one. "Not to spoil your moment here, but could you get to the more pressing information?"

"Oh, sure. Abner did come into some money and he meant for me to have some of it."

"Great. How did those brothers find out?"

"It doesn't say," she replied with a shrug. "But there are a few more things."

"Anything that we need to know in order to survive the next few minutes?"

"Well . . . I don't suppose so."

"Then grab your rifle because we're about to have some houseguests."

Olivia folded the bundle into thirds until it was back down to the size it had been when she'd found it. Rather than concern herself with all that twine, she wedged the bundle under the sash tied around her waist. The leather cover fit snugly against her hip.

Olivia rushed to her horse and removed the rifle from the boot of her own saddle. Unlike Clint's rifle, hers was an older-model hunting rifle that had obviously been left to fend for itself in the elements.

"How much longer until they get here?" she asked.

"Not long," Clint replied. "They're riding in pretty fast. Just get behind a wall and keep your head down while I fire the first . . . hey!" Clint stopped short when he saw Olivia doing the exact opposite of what he'd just told her to do. "Where the hell do you think you're going?"

Olivia held the rifle with the stock under one arm as she reached out for the clay jar with her free hand. "We've got a bet going, remember?"

"Forget about that. Just . . . aww, hell."

Clint could tell she wasn't going to forget about anything. She already had the urn in her grasp and was running toward one of the broken walls that opened toward the nearby river. Although most of the house was still between her and the approaching riders, Clint propped his rifle on the windowsill and sighted along its barrel. If he couldn't stop her, the least he could do was cover her.

As Olivia covered the short distance between the house and the bank of the Rio Grande, she was smiling like a child who'd broken free of her parents. She set her rifle down so she could hold the urn in both hands and raise it over her head.

"I love you, Uncle Abner," she said. And with an even wider smile, she brought the urn smashing down upon a rock.

Either the sound of that shattering clay or the sight of her running to the river attracted the attention that Clint had been hoping to avoid. A shot cracked through the air, followed by a few more from the horsemen.

Clint sighted in on the puffs of smoke that had shown up around two of the riders. Since he knew the horses were too far away and moving too fast for anyone to get an accurate shot from their saddles, he took his time and held off a few seconds before squeezing his trigger.

"Whatever you're doing, do it quick," Clint shouted over his shoulder.

Kneeling on the muddy riverbank, Olivia held the two largest chunks of the urn as if they were the halves of a huge, broken egg. Ashes spilled from both halves, so she snapped her arms out to send the urn's contents toward the water.

Dusty smoke billowed from the urn, and was carried by the wind toward the sprawling river. Some of the larger bits dropped into the water, while a few stubborn pieces clattered against the remains of the urn.

Another shot came from the other end of the settlement. This time, Olivia could hear the hiss of lead whipping through the air to her right. She could hear the horses as well as they raced toward Coldwater Rock. Wilson Nagle's distinctive voice drifted to her ears, but Olivia couldn't make out exactly what he was saying.

"Get back in here!" Clint demanded as he fired a shot of his own.

Olivia took the left half of the urn and turned it over so the rest of the ashes spilled into the water. Rather than shake it out, she tossed the broken clay in as well. When she shook the right half, the clatter that had always been there was even louder. It actually sounded louder than it should have and, against her better judgment, she looked inside to see what was making all that noise.

"All right!" Clint shouted after he fired another shot at each of the riders in turn. "You won the bet! You scattered the ashes before they got here. Now just get back here before I need to scatter *you* into that damn river!"

Olivia dipped her hand into the cracked half of the urn and fished out the small key that had been clattering against the clay. "I think I've just won more than our bet," she said breathlessly.

FORTY-TWO

The four riders swooped in from the top of the rise in a formation that held together well enough for Clint to wonder if the men were the Nagles after all. Once the bullets from Clint's rifle got close enough to be felt by the riders, however, they scattered and turned just as Clint had been expecting.

More shots were fired. More commands were shouted. Finally, some obscenities were tossed at the house where Clint and Olivia waited.

"Hand over that money or we'll kill you and take it ourselves!" Boris shouted. "You're dead if you fire one more goddamn shot!"

Clint kept his back to the wall as he reloaded his rifle. "What've you got there?" he asked Olivia.

Holding out the key, she said, "I think I just found the money everyone's after."

"What's that a key to?"

"Probably the strongbox in that hole in the floor," she replied.

One of the shots from outside got close enough to blast a chunk from the windowsill over Clint's head. He ducked down a bit lower, but didn't take his eyes from her.

"What strongbox?" he asked. "I thought there was just that letter."

"There's a strongbox, but no key. I took the letter and didn't worry about the rest because I didn't want to waste enough time to get us killed."

Another couple of shots hissed through the air over their heads and punched into the walls around them.

"Too late for that," Clint said with a smirk.

"Well, maybe I thought if nobody knew about that box, those assholes outside would just leave," she said. "Or maybe this whole thing would just blow over. I don't know. Thinking about that money right then felt like a disgrace to my uncle's memory. Especially after—"

One of the riders' bullets found something metal and sparked off it to ricochet into another wall.

"Especially after reading that letter," Olivia said. "There's something else in the letter that I should tell you."

Clint shook his head and held out a hand as if that was the only way to get her to stop. Once she bit her tongue, he told her, "You can tell me this later. Right now, we need to say hello to our guests. Their horses are going to be within pistol range any second."

Olivia raised herself up a bit and craned her neck before Clint took her by the arm and pulled her down again. She hit the floor on her backside and said, "They're right outside."

Clint did the one thing that could take Olivia completely off guard at that moment. He gathered his feet beneath him so he was crouched against the wall instead of sitting against it, let out a breath, and smiled. "All right," he said as he held the rifle across his chest. "Now's when the fun begins."

FORTY-THREE

The first horse to reach Abner's house thundered to within a few feet of the wall and then skidded to a stop. The rider swung down from the saddle, landed hard on both feet, and pulled the trigger of the gun in his fist. He stepped through the crumbling doorway, looked for a target, and caught the stock of Clint's rifle in his face.

Stepping into the doorway, Clint took a quick look at the gunman and then slammed his boot into the man's chest. He didn't recognize the gunman's face, but knew the Nagles weren't far behind him. He could hear the brothers shouting orders back and forth like a couple of feuding generals.

"There he is!" Boris said. "Shoot the son of a bitch!"

Now that he was in the doorway, Clint could see where the others were. One horse stood just outside the house, its rider still lying on the ground, trying to catch his breath. Another horse was being ridden around the back of the house, while two more were closer to what Clint had figured was a small livery.

One rider let out a sharp yell to his horse and got the animal moving toward the house. Clint didn't recognize that one's face either, but he didn't have any trouble recognizing the gun in the rider's hand. As soon as he saw the rider take aim at him, Clint brought up his rifle and pulled his trigger.

That shot blazed through the air and knocked the rider from his saddle. While the man was kicking and flailing on his way to the ground, Clint had already levered in a fresh round and fired the rifle again. The second bullet clipped the rider's chest and slapped the upper portion of his body to the ground before his legs could hit the dirt.

When he landed, the gunman tossed his pistol and let out a pained groan.

"Murdering bastard!" Boris yelled as he hopped down from his horse and ran for cover inside the livery.

Clint stepped over the gunman he'd knocked from the doorway and transferred his rifle to his left hand. After propping the rifle onto his shoulder, Clint circled around toward the right side of the livery.

"Hiring men to do your fighting now, Boris?" Clint asked. "I guess you haven't had much luck on your own. Come to think of it, you haven't even had that much luck with Olivia. I hear she worked you over pretty good with a shovel."

That worked better than Clint had hoped.

Not only did Boris show where he was hiding, but he did so with enough bluster to draw the aim of a blind man.

"I don't give a fuck who you are!" Boris snarled as he exploded from the livery. "You ain't touching that money!"

All Clint needed to do was step to his right to get out of Boris's line of fire. Boris pulled the trigger of his .44 again and again, but only managed to blast a few holes into the corner of the livery. Before he'd delivered his sixth shot, Boris drew his second pistol and started firing that one as well.

Boris gritted his teeth and worked his way along the front of the livery. He emptied half of his second pistol before reaching the corner. When he rounded the corner, Boris fired a shot before he could even get a look at Clint.

That shot, just like all the ones before it, hit nothing but wall.

Clint wasn't there.

As Boris looked around, he didn't see any trace of Clint. "Son of a bitch," he muttered.

The moment he heard something move, Boris slammed his back against the wall and fired another shot in that direction.

There was still nothing, so Boris fumbled his cylinder open so he could reload his first gun.

Something moved again. This time, however, Boris could tell the movement was coming from inside the livery behind him. "Hey!" Boris shouted to the gunman who'd been kicked to the ground in Abner's doorway.

The gunman got to his knees and then climbed to his feet. Blood streamed down his face from that first hit from the stock of Clint's rifle, so he swiped at it with the back of his hand.

"Where'd Adams go?" Boris shouted.

"Who?" the gunman asked.

"The man who knocked you down. Where'd he go?"

"I was about to shoot him when you came charging out of there," the gunman replied. "If you wouldn't have moved, I could have—"

"Just keep your eyes open," Boris snapped.

Suddenly, the gunman let out a surprised grunt and stabbed a finger toward the livery.

Boris nodded and turned to look through one of the holes that had rotted through the wall. Not only did he see Clint, but Boris found himself looking straight down the barrel of Clint's pistol. Boris's next move was to take a shot at Clint while he could.

Clint pulled his trigger just as Boris lifted his gun arm.

The bullet sped through the hole in the wall and caught Boris in the chest to drill a hole through his heart.

The gunman who'd just stood up fired a quick shot at Clint, which came within inches of drawing Clint's blood.

After snapping his arm out like a whip, Clint aimed at the remaining gunman and sent a round into the man's eye. Once more, the gunman was knocked to the ground. This time, he didn't get up.

FORTY-FOUR

Olivia huddled in the narrow corner as if she still had un-broken walls on all sides of her. Instead, there was barely enough wall in front of her to keep her partially hidden. The sounds of gunshots exploded through the air, but she intended on staying put as Clint had asked.

She heard shouting, but didn't move.

She heard more shots and what had to have been a man's dying breath, but Olivia still didn't move.

When she heard steps knock against the battered floor, Olivia tightened her grip on her rifle and hoped to see Clint step into her sight.

The man who peeked in at her wasn't Clint.

"There you are," Wilson said in a dry, almost singsong voice. "If there was anything to be found in here, I knew you'd be right beside it."

"There's nothing here," Olivia said as she aimed her rifle at him. "Just leave me alone!"

Wilson stopped coming forward, but leered at her as if he was somehow drawing her to him. His smile had frozen on to his face like something that had been chipped into a statue. Even as the gunshots continued to be fired outside, Wilson acted as if he didn't hear a single one of them.

"Whatever you got in there, just hand it over," he said.

Olivia shook her head. "There's nothing here! All I meant to do was scatter Abner's ashes. That's the only reason we're here."

"Then why hire a man like Clint Adams?"

"To protect me from you!" she snapped. "You and your idiot brother don't even need a reason to hurt someone. Since you got it in your heads that there's money to be had, you're like a rash."

Wilson laughed and nodded. "A rash. I like that."

"What are you doing?" Olivia asked nervously.

Holding his pistol in front of him, Wilson slowly opened the cylinder and checked each round. "Just making sure this is ready to blast a hole through your head."

Olivia raised her rifle in trembling hands. "I'll kill you first."

"Yeah? Well, now's your chance."

Keeping his eyes on her, Wilson held his pistol so Olivia could see it from the side. After a few seconds, he snapped the cylinder shut with a flick of his wrist. He shook his head and said, "I knew you didn't have it in you to fire. That ain't nothing to be ashamed of. After all, it's only money."

"Even if there was money, it's not yours."

"My brother and I stayed when you left to go see the world. We probably knew Abner better than you did. Do you know we even helped him make repairs to his house when he was ill?"

"You're crazy," Olivia whispered. She could feel a cold sweat breaking on her brow and her arms losing the strength they needed to keep the rifle pointed at Wilson. "That's all just crazy talk."

"All right then," Wilson sighed. "Abner always had money and we didn't. You went out and made a life for yourself when we couldn't. Your family always got all the good chances and we didn't. Now that one of your kin has turned on you, none of you deserves one goddamned dime. We're taking this money and there ain't a damn thing to do about it, so pull that trigger or I'll take that rifle right out of your hands."

Olivia steeled herself and pressed the rifle against her shoulder. She held her breath so she could use all of her strength to take aim and pull her trigger. Her mind raced with a hundred good reasons why she should fire.

Her life depended on it.

Suddenly, Wilson's hand snapped out to take hold of the rifle's barrel. Before she could do anything about it, Olivia felt the rifle get twisted until her finger snapped beneath the trigger guard. The pain only got worse as Wilson roughly yanked the rifle away from her.

"You had your chance, Olivia," Wilson said. "Two of them. You wasted them both. I've got the chance to get rich and I also just got the chance to shove this rifle up into you and pull the trigger just to see what happens. I ain't wasting neither of my chances."

Olivia grabbed her hand and held it tight. She could feel the broken bones of her finger, but she no longer felt the pain. As she let out her breath, she whispered a few soft words.

"Oh, thank God."

Wilson's brow furrowed when he heard that. He still had a confused look on his face when he heard the scrape of a boot against the floor at the back of the house. Turning to the left, he found Clint standing at the section of broken wall that opened to the Rio Grande.

Firing both the rifle and his pistol at the same time, Wilson sent a wave of lead toward that half of the house.

Clint dropped down and dove so Wilson would have to turn even farther away from Olivia to follow him. Wilson did just that, and corrected his aim even quicker than Clint had anticipated.

A bullet ripped through Clint's collar and dug into his

neck like a hot claw. The modified Colt bucked against Clint's palm to put a round into Wilson's chest.

Wilson twitched as the bullet punched through him, but didn't drop. He clenched his jaw against the pain and kept firing. Just then, another pop could be heard and Wilson twitched again. He turned around to find Olivia aiming her smoking derringer at him. Because she needed to hold the little gun in her left hand, she'd only been able to graze the fatty portion of Wilson's gut.

Still twitching with a combination of rage and pain, Wilson growled, "You bitch." Before he could do anything more than that, a pair of bullets from Clint's pistol knocked Wilson off his feet and sent him staggering into a corner. By the time he slumped to the floor, Wilson was dead.

"Sorry about that," Clint said as he stepped forward. "I thought you got him."

"I wish I had been the one to finish him off," Olivia said. "But thanks for being there."

Clint helped her up and then reloaded his Colt.

"Are there any more?" she asked.

"If there were supposed to be any more, they turned tail and ran. From what I saw of these other two, the Nagle brothers probably just hired them off a street corner or in a saloon somewhere. Now, what about that lockbox?"

Olivia set her rifle down and removed the leather bundle from her sash. "First of all, you should read this for yourself," she said as she handed the letter from under the floorboard to Clint.

"You sure you want me to read this?"

"Yes. You've been through enough to help me. I think you should know how this ends. Besides, I might still need you to come with me on one more train ride if you don't mind."

Before he agreed or disagreed to that ride, Clint opened the letter. It read:

My dearest little bird,

I have tried to be a good uncle, but I'm not the best man. I've made plenty of mistakes, but have also had some things pan out recently. I know I might meet my end soon, but there's no need to tell you that because by now I will already be gone. A man in my spot learns that the only real thing that matters is loved ones you can trust.

Since our family has been whittled down one way or another over the years, whatever I've got left will be split up among you. But when there's that much money involved, there's bound to be some backstabbing. I hope this isn't the case, but it usually is. To this end, I've devised a little test.

First of all, I've arranged to notify you and Jenny about my passing. I hope at least one of the letters I paid to have sent were delivered without too much trouble. Secondly, I've already had my safe delivered to Jenny's house in Dallas. She's the only one who stays put, Olivia, so don't get your nose bent out of joint.

Olivia, you should have been told to scatter my ashes here, so get to it. While you're at it, don't forget to check your nest for eggs. If all goes right, you'll be able to open the safe and I trust you'll split the money fairly. If one of you tries to disgrace my memory, the other will get the money. If Jenny tries anything rotten, you fly away, Olivia, and live your life. Some money isn't worth facing that sort of ugliness. Hopefully, you'll both do just fine together and will end up rich. At least I could provide for my loved ones in some way.

Whatever happens, I trust you'll know what to do.

Love,
Abner

When Clint looked up from the letter, he saw Olivia holding a key.

"There's a strongbox in that hole," she told him. With that, she knelt over the space where the floorboard had been removed and pulled out a small iron box. The dusty key in her hand fit into the box and she opened the lid.

"What is it?" Clint asked.

The box contained only one thing. "This," Olivia replied as she pulled out a larger key, "means we need to go back to Dallas."

FORTY-FIVE

A short ride and a few train stations later, Clint and Olivia were back on Jenny's doorstep. Clint knocked and stood with his hand on his holstered Colt as Jenny opened the door. She had to blink several times before she could form enough words to greet them.

"Oh," Jenny stammered. "I . . . welcome back."

"What's the matter, Jenny?" Olivia asked as she stepped around Clint and walked into the house. "Weren't you expecting us?"

"Yes. Of course I was."

"Where's the safe?"

"What?" Jenny asked.

Olivia cocked her head and looked as if she wanted to spit in the woman's round face. "Abner's safe. I know it's here."

"I don't know what you're talking about."

"All right then," Olivia said as she reached into her pocket and removed the large key that had been in the hidden strongbox. "Then you won't be needing this."

Jenny waited for all of three seconds before she finally snapped her hand out to try and take the key from Olivia. Although Olivia was taken by surprise by Jenny's speed, Clint was quick enough to grab Jenny's wrist.

When she felt her fingertips graze the key, Jenny let out a grunt that sounded more like it had come from a hungry animal. "Give me that! Abner wanted me to have that money!"

"He wanted us both to have it," Olivia said. "I got a letter saying so, and I'm sure you did, too."

"My letter said that I was to give you his ashes and wait for you to come back with the key. Until then, I was to hide the safe just in case you tried to take the money for yourself."

"Abner was a smart man."

"He was a fool," Jenny spat. "He didn't even put the right key into those ashes."

Now it was Clint's turn to be surprised. "You dug through those ashes before we even got here?"

Looking up at him with a disgusted expression on her face, Jenny replied, "Sure I did. There was something in there, but the key was too small for the damn lock."

"Seems like Abner was even smarter than I thought," Olivia said.

"Yes, but he loved you," Jenny said. "If anyone was to get preferential treatment even after he was dead, it was you."

"Is that why you hired the Nagles to follow me?" Olivia asked.

Jenny showed her a smug grin and said, "I wouldn't dream of doing such a thing."

"Bullshit. Wilson mentioned one of my own kin was turning on me."

"Why would he say something like that?"

"Because he thought I wasn't going to live long enough for it to make any difference. Also, you're the only one who knew about the money, where to find me, and how to find the Nagles."

That caused the grin on Jenny's face to dry up. Then she started to squirm against Clint's grip. "Let go of my arm," she demanded.

"I don't think you're in a spot to make demands," he replied.

Olivia patted Clint's shoulder and told him, "Go ahead and let her go. Jenny, show me that safe."

The moment Clint turned her loose, Jenny walked over to a small table in the corner of her dining room. She removed the vase of flowers and cloth from the table to reveal it was actually a safe that was roughly twice the size of a footstool.

Olivia walked over to the safe, fitted the key into the lock, and turned it. When the door swung open, there were neat stacks of money piled almost to the top of the safe's innards. After taking a moment to look at the money, Olivia spread the tablecloth on the floor and stacked a close approximation of half that money on it.

"There," Olivia said as she gathered up the tablecloth to form a makeshift sack for the money. "The rest is yours."

"What?" Clint asked.

Although she didn't say anything, Jenny looked even more surprised.

"The other half is yours, Jenny," Olivia repeated. "It's what Abner wanted. He hoped we'd just scatter those ashes, visit that house, and open the safe. He wanted to provide for us. That was his dying wish, so that's how it's going to be."

Jenny blinked and looked at Clint as if she expected him to shoot her. When Clint didn't make a move in that direction, Jenny opened her arms and walked toward Olivia. "I'm so sorry, sweetie. I don't know what came over me. Times have been hard and—"

"Shut up," Olivia said as she stood up and picked up the money. "Don't ever talk to me again. As far as I'm concerned, you're dead."

"I understand. If you ever need anything, you know where to find me."

"I better not know where to find you." Stopping short of the front door, Olivia added, "Because the Nagle brothers had a few cousins who were just as rough as Boris and Wilson. I intend on sending word to them about how you got those two killed. They're a tightly knit group, so I suppose they won't like hearing about that."

"What?" Jenny gasped. "You can't do that!"

After taking a moment to let that sink in, Olivia walked through the door. Clint tipped his hat to Jenny, stepped outside, and shut the door behind him.

"If Jenny did send those killers after us, you might want to hand her over to the law," Clint said.

"No," Olivia replied. "Jenny made her bed, so she'll have to lie in it. I'm through with her, and you've already done more than enough. Do you think you could help me with one last thing?"

"What is it?"

"There's a few more Nagles I need to find."

Watch for

THE MADAME OF SILVER JUNCTION

315th novel in the exciting GUNSMITH series
from Jove

Coming in March!

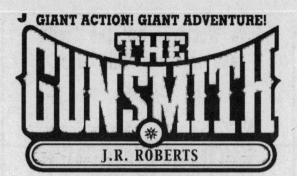

GIANT ACTION! GIANT ADVENTURE!

THE GUNSMITH

J.R. ROBERTS

penguin.com

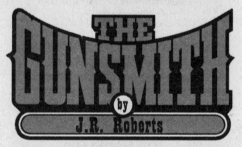

Presents

Great Inspirational Romance at a Great Price!

Heartsong Presents books are inspirational romances in contemporary and historical settings, designed to give you an enjoyable, spirit-lifting reading experience. You can choose wonderfully written titles from some of today's best authors like Wanda E. Brunstetter, Mary Connealy, Susan Page Davis, Cathy Marie Hake, Joyce Livingston, and many others.

When ordering quantities less than twelve, above titles are $2.97 each.
Not all titles may be available at time of order.

HP653	Lakeside, M. Davis	HP713	Secondhand Heart, J. Livingston
HP654	Alaska Summer, M. H. Flinkman	HP714	Anna's Journey, N. Toback
HP657	Love Worth Finding, C. M. Hake	HP717	Merely Players, K. Kovach
HP658	Love Worth Keeping, J. Livingston	HP718	In His Will, C. Hake
HP665	Bah Humbug, Mrs. Scrooge,	HP721	Through His Grace, K. Hake
	J. Livingston	HP722	Christmas Mommy, T. Fowler
HP666	Sweet Charity, J. Thompson	HP726	Promising Angela, K. V. Sawyer
HP669	The Island, M. Davis	HP729	Bay Hideaway, B. Loughner
HP670	Miss Menace, N. Lavo	HP730	With Open Arms, J. L. Barton
HP673	Flash Flood, D. Mills	HP733	Safe in His Arms, T. Davis
HP677	Banking on Love, J. Thompson	HP734	Larkspur Dreams, A. Higman and
HP678	Lambert's Peace, R. Hauck		J. A. Thompson
HP681	The Wish, L. Bliss	HP737	Darcy's Inheritance, L. Ford
HP682	The Grand Hotel, M. Davis	HP738	Picket Fence Pursuit, J. Johnson
HP685	Thunder Bay, B. Loughner	HP741	The Heart of the Matter, K. Dykes
HP689	Unforgettable, J. L. Barton	HP742	Prescription for Love, A. Boeshaar
HP690	Heritage, M. Davis	HP745	Family Reunion, J. L. Barton
HP693	Dear John, K. V. Sawyer	HP746	By Love Acquitted, Y. Lehman
HP694	Riches of the Heart, T. Davis	HP749	Love by the Yard, G. Sattler
HP697	Dear Granny, P. Griffin	HP750	Except for Grace, T. Fowler
HP698	With a Mother's Heart, J. Livingston	HP753	Long Trail to Love, P. Griffin
HP701	Cry of My Heart, L. Ford	HP754	Red Like Crimson, J. Thompson
HP702	Never Say Never, L. N. Dooley	HP757	Everlasting Love, L. Ford
HP705	Listening to Her Heart, J. Livingston	HP758	Wedded Bliss, K. Y'Barbo
HP706	The Dwelling Place, K. Miller	HP761	Double Blessing, D. Mayne
HP709	That Wilder Boy, K. V. Sawyer	HP762	Photo Op, L. A. Coleman
HP710	To Love Again, J. L. Barton	HP765	Sweet Sugared Love, P. Griffin
		HP766	Pursuing the Goal, J. Johnson

SEND TO: **Heartsong Presents** Readers' Service
P.O. Box 721, Uhrichsville, Ohio 44683

Please send me the items checked above. I am enclosing $ _____
(please add $3.00 to cover postage per order. OH add 7% tax. NJ add 6%). Send check or money order, no cash or C.O.D.s, please.
To place a credit card order, call 1-740-922-7280.

NAME _____

ADDRESS _____

CITY/STATE _____ ZIP _____

HP 12-07

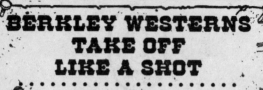

BERKLEY WESTERNS TAKE OFF LIKE A SHOT